HER A   HEALERS

SUSAN HAYES

ABOUT THE BOOK

She's ready to move on to the next chapter of her life — She just never expected it would be a love story.

Jodi Clark has been many things over the years: a doctor, a wife, and a divorced single mother. Now, there's just one more thing she needs to do – for once in her life, she's going to put herself first.

An unexpected invitation to Haven colony comes at the perfect moment. A new home and new challenges are just what she needs to kick-start her time of self-discovery. At least, that's what she thought...

Haven isn't as peaceful as its name implies. There are hidden threats, secret societies, and most dangerous of all, a pair of sexy alien silver foxes that are as alluring as they are off-limits.

Two alien healers who cannot mend their broken hearts are about to meet their cure...

Tariq and Sulat are Vardarian *anrik*, blood-bound

brothers destined to share their lives, a family, and a mate. When a tragic accident claimed the life of their *mahaya*, grief shattered their lives and ended their hopes for the future.

Joining the exodus to Haven seems like the best way to move forward and rebuild what remains of their family. Their new home is indeed a haven, but one under threat from outside forces and the pressures of traditions best left in the past.

Three healers willing to risk their lives to protect their patients... but do they have the courage to risk their hearts?

PROLOGUE

Beyond the edge of civilized space is a newly colonized planet. It's a haven for the homeless, the hopeful, and those dreaming of freedom.

The beings who live here might be different species from vastly different worlds - but they all have one thing in common. Whoever they are, and wherever they came from, Haven is now their home.

The land is uncharted. The dangers are unknown. It's a world full of possibilities – for those willing to risk everything.

Welcome to Haven Colony.

1

Jody scanned the faces of the women watching her. All of them were engaged and curious, though she spotted a few thoughtful expressions and even a couple of confused ones scattered throughout the room.

"Does anyone have any questions?" she asked.

Hands shot into the air before she even finished her sentence. This group of colonists from Earth's slowly dying hive cities were some of the most eager students she'd ever had. They were also woefully lacking in basic knowledge about how their bodies worked.

Today, they were gathered in one of the utilitarian rooms that were the norm in this part of the colony. All the buildings had been donated by the military, meaning they were nondescript, prefabricated structures. Functional, practical, and uniform in every way without a hint of creativity or comfortable touches. It reminded her of her ex-husband, Kyle—a military man down to his disciplined and squared-away soul.

She left thoughts of the ancient past behind and

focused on the needs of the present. One by one, she answered their questions, correcting misconceptions and addressing concerns. These women had all been selected for their adaptability and willingness to learn, and they were all eager to fill in any gaps in their education. Gaps that only existed because they'd been too busy trying to survive to do anything else.

"Dr. Clark. I, uh, have one more question." Neda's cheeks darkened as she spoke, and her fingers tugged nervously at the sleeve of the blue and gray jumpsuit most of them chose to wear.

"Ask it." Jody suspected she knew what was coming. Vixi had given her a heads up about a new rumor moving through the group of recent arrivals.

"It's about the Vardarians."

Jody nodded. "I'm not an expert on them by any means. I've only been here a few weeks longer than all of you, but I will do my best to answer your question."

Neda acknowledged her statement but didn't speak for several seconds. Instead, she glanced around at her fellow colonists as if seeking support. Several of them smiled or nodded back.

So this was a group question and Neda was their spokesperson. This had to be about the rumor.

"I, uh." Neda looked down and then back up at Jody. "I heard that the Vardarian men like, well, um, doing it to a woman at the same time. You know. Both holes. At once."

Jody waited, but Neda didn't continue. "Before I address what you said, do you have a question, or are you looking for confirmation?"

"They're bigger than us," Amy piped up. "I mean, taller. Broader. So they must have bigger dicks, too. How does that work with a human female? Won't that hurt?"

Several women tittered while others leaned forward in their chairs, eager to hear the explanation.

Jody made a note to thank Vixi for warning her this might come up. The Vardarian healer had traveled to Earth and back twice now, both times to pick up female colonists and bring them to the colony. Despite the time they'd spent with the female Vardarians on board, there were some things the human women still felt more comfortable asking another human. That was one of the reasons Jody had been invited to work at the colony. They needed a human doctor to tend to the colonists coming from Earth.

Jody gave them a moment to compose themselves before answering. "Double penetration is a personal choice. From what I understand, it's more common in multi-partner relationships. But it is a *choice*. One that all the partners agree to."

Now she had their rapt attention. "As for the physical side of things, I can confirm that yes, they are larger than human males in every aspect." She raised her hands. "Not that I have any personal experience with that. But I've done some book-based research."

They all laughed at that, easing some of the tension that had crept into the room.

"Regarding the rest of your question. There are ways of making that kind of thing easier. Preparation. *Uli* oil, which we'll be talking about next week, and trust." She looked around the room again. "No matter what kind of sex you're having, being able to trust your partner, or partners, will make it more enjoyable. That's why none of the males are allowed to enter this camp yet. We want to be sure you are all comfortable and confident before you meet with them."

Murmurings and side conversations started up and then died as Amy spoke up again. "That's great for us, Dr. Clark, but what about you and Lores? You're both human and you're already living with the Vardarians. Aren't you worried someone will catch your scent and boom, you're married?"

"Mated," Jody corrected. "And no, I'm not worried. If it happens, it happens." She shrugged. "But I don't think it will. Most of the healers I work with are mated. That means they have no interest in anyone but their mates."

She looked to the back of the room where her friend and associate, Lores, lurked near the door. She'd arrived about ten minutes ago, but so far, no one else had noticed.

Lores grinned and picked up the narrative. "I wouldn't complain if a pair of those hot aliens announced they were my *mahoyen*. So far, no luck, though."

Everyone turned to look at her. "You're not worried about it?" Sanji asked.

Lores snorted. "Worried? About having two sexy alien males hot for my body and looking for a lifetime of orgasms and commitment? Hell no!" She spread her arms. "Bring it on! I may have gray hair and plenty of miles on this chassis, but I'm not dead yet. And if I die in bed with two hot-blooded males? I can't think of a better way to go."

The room erupted into laughter again, creating the

Chapter 1

perfect moment to end the session. Once it had quieted down a little, Jody sent them on their way.

Once the room emptied out, Lores cocked her head to one side and looked at her with a quizzical expression. "What was that about all the males you work with being mated? Some of them are single."

"Sulat and Tariq might have lost their *mahaya*, but they are not single.

They're grieving the loss of their soulmate. I cannot imagine what that's like. To find the one person you're destined for and then have them snatched away."

"It would be rough," Lores agreed. "But from what I understand, most Vardarians in their situation eventually find someone else. It's never the same, of course. But love comes in many forms and flavors."

"That's not the point. Even if they were available, we need to work together as professionals. That means they're off limits."

"Maybe. But they're also handsome, smart, and sexy as hell." Lores pointed a playful finger in her direction. "And don't try to tell me you haven't noticed."

"Oh, I've noticed. But that doesn't change anything. Besides, we've barely exchanged more than a few words. I'm busy with the colonists and taking care of our other patients."

"You mean the cranky preggers princess and our newly remade cyber-jockey Jade? Please. Jade has made a full recovery, and Phaedra is doing well. She just hates being cooped up. Even if it is for her and the baby's protection." Lores grinned wryly. "I figure if it weren't for the baby, she'd have broken out by now. That girl never met a rule she didn't want to break into a million pieces."

"Says the woman who helped implant her with black market tech. From what I've heard from you and Phae, back then you were just as bad as she is."

Her friend's grin widened, the expression deepening the lines around her eyes and mouth. "Still am, thank you very much. I'm just better at hiding it now. With age comes wisdom. Which means that since I'm older than you, I'm also wiser. There's something between you, Tariq, and Sulat. Don't ignore it because you think you know what they want. Let *them* make that decision."

Jody acknowledged her friend's advice, even though she didn't believe it. The two males were cordial, professional, and entirely disinterested in her as a woman. She didn't take that personally. They had no interest in any female as far as she could tell. And the holographic AI that acted as clinic manager and virtual medical assistant had been programmed by their deceased mate.

She'd recently learned that Rae even *looked* exactly like her creator. The program was only an echo of the female they'd loved, but it was obvious they had no intention of moving on.

She respected their choice. Besides, she hadn't come to Haven to get laid or mated. She was here because it was time to start a new chapter in her life and discover who she was now that her son was an adult. Jake had followed his father's path and joined the military. That was another decision she had to accept, even if she didn't like it.

"You've got that look again," Lores said, her tone softer now. "Thinking about Jacob?"

"Always." Jody smiled. "Every time I think about choices, it reminds me that my son, who could have been anything he wanted to be, went into the AIF, just to gain some sliver of his father's attention. I wish he'd done something else. Anything else."

"I know you do. But that boy is as stubborn as his momma. He'll be fine, Jody. Stop worrying and remember why we came here."

They'd had this conversation many times, but Jody asked anyway. It was a ritual now, one they both enjoyed. "Can you remind me again why you dragged me to the brink of known space?"

Her friend of more than a decade grinned at her and winked. "We're here to help others and enjoy ourselves. Clean air, fresh water, good food, and friends. That's why we're here." Then she waggled her brows. "And I'm hoping to enjoy the attentions of some of the local wildlife. Cyborgs and Vardarians, oh my." She fanned her face and laughed.

Jody nodded. "I will admit, the scenery around here is quite lovely."

"Now that's better. Relax. Enjoy yourself a little. In fact, that's what we're going to do now. Come on. We've got time to grab lunch before we're due back at the clinic."

"You mean you want to go ogle the eye candy while we eat? Let me guess. We're going to the Bar None?"

"You know it." Lores chuckled as she led the way outside. "Like I said earlier. I may be old, but I'm not dead yet. I know what I like, and I'm enjoying myself. You should try it sometime."

Jody stayed silent this time. She wanted to follow her friend's advice, but that wasn't so easy when the only males she wanted were out of her reach.

2

Sulat's office wasn't large. He couldn't even stretch his wings properly in it, but it wasn't a place he spent much time, so he made do. He'd sacrificed space here to extend his lab by a few extra meters. That's where he preferred to be, but lately he'd found reasons to work from his office. It meant he was close enough to keep an eye on Tariq. His *anrik* wasn't himself lately, and he wasn't sure what the problem was. Work? Worry? Or something else? He needed to know, and Tariq refused to talk about it. In fact, lately Tariq hadn't spoken much at all.

At the moment, his blood-bonded brother was in his office across the hall. He should be working, but all Sulat heard from that area was the rustle of wings, irritated grunts, and the occasional sigh.

It only took a moment to confirm they had no patients scheduled for the next two hours.

Good. It was time to go face the grumpy *gharshtu* and

find out what the problem was. This time, he wouldn't back down until he got some answers.

He was halfway to Tariq's door when a chime sounded, announcing someone had entered the med-clinic.

He growled in near silent frustration at the interruption but broke into a grin when he heard a familiar voice call out from the waiting room. "Hey, Rae. Are they here? Hello?"

"Vixi, we're both back here," he answered, his previous annoyance evaporating with the arrival of their daughter.

He and Tariq met her in the hall between their offices. She hugged him first and then turned to hug Tariq. The moment her slender arms wrapped around his waist, she sighed, her lovely face scrunching into a frown that reminded him of her mother.

"You promised me you were going to eat more, Dad."

This was news to Sulat, but he wasn't surprised she hadn't mentioned it to him. Vixi had been raised to respect the privacy of others, especially in matters of health and wellness.

"I am eating," Tariq protested and looked over at him. "Tell her, Sulat."

"He eats if I remind him. I imagine there's a barely touched plate of food on his desk right now. I put it there an hour ago." He was in no mood to cover for his *anrik*. In fact, Vixi might be the ally he needed in the coming confrontation with Tariq. The male was as stubborn as a *mogat*. Raenia was the only one who could manage him when he got like this. If she were here, she'd tease and cajole the truth out of him.

The brief thought of their beloved *mahaya* made his heart ache. She'd been gone for several years now, and her absence had left a hole in their lives and their souls. As deeply as he mourned her passing, he knew Tariq carried the heavier burden. His grief was tangled up in guilt, despite the fact no one could have done anything to change what happened.

Vixi leaned back and peered into Tariq's office. "He's right. You barely touched your meal."

Tariq winced at that and Sulat had to hide his smile. Their daughter had landed a direct hit and given him the opening he needed.

"You can't keep doing this to yourself." Sulat moved closer to drop a friendly hand on his *anrik's* shoulder to take the sting out of his words. "You barely eat. You never laugh. The only time you smile is when our little whirlwind pays us a visit. You never let it affect your work, but at home it's like I am living with two ghosts instead of one."

He hadn't intended to say that last bit, but the thought had been in the back of his mind for weeks. It spilled out before he could stop himself.

All three of them froze for several long seconds.

"*Bakaffa*," Tariq snarled and pulled away from Sulat's hand.

"Hey! No calling him an asshole," Vixi scolded before turning her attention his way. "And you could try to be kinder. This isn't easy for any of us."

Her voice cracked at the end, reminding him that

Vixi carried her own grief at the loss of her mother. Guilt sank its claws into his heart and squeezed. This wasn't going well.

"I apologize. I'm worried about you, Riq."

"*Atarflorinti*," Vixi said.

"Witnessed and accepted," Tariq said a half-second later, his tone only slightly grudging.

Vixi stepped back and glared at them both. "Is this what you two are like when I'm not around?"

"Sometimes," they both said at the same time.

"That's better."

Tariq looked down at their daughter with a bemused expression. "When did our little whirlwind surpass us in maturity?"

"About five minutes ago, and I'm not enjoying the experience. So will the two of you please fix whatever this is?" she retorted.

"That's going to be a longer conversation. One that should involve chairs and *varyn*."

Tariq actually smiled a little. "You're not playing fair. You know that's my favorite drink. Wait, how did you get the ingredients? I haven't found anyone who will import it."

"I found someone. Well, Vixi did. I just approached them with an offer."

Vixi beamed. "Hezza B agreed? What did that cost you?"

"Let's just say that she's a very shrewd negotiator and leave it at that." The price had been steep, but he had no regrets. Some of the fruits and flowers required to brew *varyn* were a luxury even within the Vardarian empire, many light years away.

"Thank you." Tariq held out his arm to him in a gesture he hadn't used for weeks.

Sulat reached out to touch the back of his wrist to his *anrik's* so the scars from their blood-bonding ceremony touched. "Anything for you, my brother."

"Rae, please engage the privacy protocol for this area. You know what to do if anyone drops by without an appointment."

Rae's hologram appeared near the door to the waiting room, somehow aware that she shouldn't intrude on the moment. The AI was Raenia's creation, and she had based the program on her appearance and personality. They were the same height and build, though Rae had altered her hairstyle after her creator's death. Her hair was the same blonde shade as Vixi's, and she had even been programmed with some of the same mannerisms as her creator. While their *mahaya* was alive, it hadn't been an issue. Now she was gone, Rae was both a comfort and a reminder of what they'd lost.

"Of course. Shall I have the dispenser create the usual array of preferred snacks?"

"Please. I think we'd all enjoy that." Vixi shot Tariq a look that was identical to the one Raenia used when she was making a point. "Won't we."

Tariq raised his wings and bowed his head in a gesture somewhere between surrender and a shrug. "I could eat. I meant to have lunch. I just got distracted."

They moved to the room they'd designated as their break room. It had windows to the back garden, plenty of natural light, and space to stretch their wings. It also had a replicator that provided an array of hot and cold meals and beverages.

As they sat down at a table, he remembered his offer. "Rae, please send a droid to retrieve the black flask from my lab's coolers. You know the one."

"Of course."

"You sneaky male. You've got it brewed and chilling already?" Tariq's tone was light and friendly, but his gaze held a hint of wariness. "This talk really has been coming for a while if you've had time to organize all this."

"The *varyn* was intended to be a surprise." Sulat shrugged. "Now seemed a good moment for it, though."

"He wanted to cheer you up." Vixi smiled at them both. "We're family. We'll always worry about each other. I know the two of you don't like it when I leave on my missions to Earth."

"That planet is not safe," Tariq stated.

"That entire sector isn't safe," Sulat said half a second later. He liked the humans he'd met well enough, but their home system had been stripped of resources and left to die along with an alarming number of beings who lacked the money or means to escape.

Vixi laughed at them. "Have you been rehearsing those lines?"

"No. But we're your fathers. It's our job to worry about you." Tariq's expression softened into one of fatherly pride. "Helping to save the females of Earth and bringing them here is admirable, but you have to admit, it's not the safest of jobs."

"And being a healer here is?" Her voice was edged with challenge. "This colony has dealt with spies and an

AI assassin that took over Rae's programming and nano-warfare. Not to mention the fact the entire Vardarian population here fell ill for the first time in their lives, including both of you."

"I'll admit that Haven isn't as peaceful as we expected," Sulat said.

"But we're still going to worry about you when you go to Earth," Tariq added.

"We won't be going back until this new group of colonists has acclimated and we've identified anyone who is a potential problem. They can come with us back to Earth or arrange for transportation elsewhere." She shook her head hard enough her jaw-length blonde hair bounced.

"Are there any in this new batch we should be concerned about?" Tariq asked.

"No. The new selection process worked. They're all adjusting well. No suspicious behavior, no personality conflicts of note, but they're being watched carefully, just in case."

They paused to gather the snacks from the food dispenser while Sulat poured them all a glass of *varyn*.

Vixi took a sip of the fizzy mixture and then set her glass down, her gaze moving from him to Tariq and back. "Now, tell me what's going on with the two of you. It feels like forever since we've had a chance to talk like this."

Sulat thought about that and realized she was right. Apart from a family dinner to celebrate her return home and hear about her mission, they'd been too busy to talk. She had her work, and they had theirs.

They spent the next hour chatting, laughing, and even reminiscing about the past. By the end, Tariq seemed more himself, laughing and even speaking about Raenia without more than a brief flash of sadness.

Sulat had to wonder if a family meeting and a chance to reconnect were all Tariq needed. They had kept to themselves more of late. Maybe too much.

Vixi must have come to the same conclusion because as they were clearing the table she stopped and turned to look at them, but her comment was directed at their AI. "Rae, how many times have my dads had social visitors while at work?"

Rae's answer was immediate. "None, excluding you."

"Uh-huh. Please check with their residential AI and find out how many visitors they've had at home."

"Privacy override, Rae," Tariq said.

"Request canceled. Data deleted."

"Really?" Vixi rustled her wings, clearly vexed. "I guess the answer to my question is the same as the first, then. None."

"We've had visitors," Sulat stated as he frantically tried to remember the last time anyone had come by just to socialize.

"Name one."

"You," he said.

"I don't count. I'm family. Try again."

"We attended the party after we'd all recovered from the outbreak," Tariq said.

"That doesn't count. The entire colony was there." She set aside the tray she held and pulled them both in for a hug. "I can't be the only being you see besides your patients. You both need to get out and make friends. That's why we came here. To start again. I'm doing that. You two seem to be stuck."

"We're not stuck. We're busy," Tariq said, sounding aggrieved.

"But you're lonely." Suddenly, her eyes lit up. It was a look they knew well, and it boded trouble.

"What are you up to?"

"Oh, nothing. I was just thinking that if you haven't had anyone over for a social call, you've not spent any time with Dr. Clark yet. She's your colleague, and the only human healer on the planet. Don't you think the three of you should get to know each other better?"

Tariq's jaw tightened and his scales shimmered a brilliant silver for a brief second.

Vixi missed it because her attention was on him at that moment, but Sulat saw it clearly. Something about the human doctor had his *anrik* on edge, but he had no idea what it could be. She was a skilled healer, kind and capable. She was also quite attractive, and it had surprised him to learn no male had claimed her.

The unmated Vardarian males would be happy to keep her company in any way she desired. He and Tariq could take a lover if they wished, but so far, Tariq had shown no interest in doing so. It was one of the reasons they'd come to Haven—to escape a growing number of available females hoping to take Raenia's place.

3

THANKS TO VIXI'S DECLARATION, Tariq spent the next week fending off suggestions from both his daughter and his *anrik* about ways to improve their social life.

Their ideas were good. Some were even things he'd considered himself, but there was one problem—he didn't *want* to do any of them. Losing Raenia had stolen too much of the light from his life, and he'd grown to like the shadows. It felt like a betrayal to his *mahaya's* memory to go back to the way things used to be... before.

The word held an almost sacred meaning now. Before the accident. Before she died. Before his world was shattered. The move to Haven was supposed to mark a clean break from the two phases of their lives, a dividing line between their past and present. It had worked, mostly. Sulat was happier and Vixi... He smiled as he picked at the meal one of the household droids had placed on the side table beside his favorite chair. Vixi had blossomed since they'd arrived here. His pride in her accomplishments could carry him through even his darkest moods, even if her current choices meant she was gone for long periods of time.

His daughter had an adventurous streak, just like her mother. He suspected the newest member of the colony's medical team was the same way. Dr. Jody Clark had worked in a variety of locations, including some of the most distant outposts and isolated space stations. She was bright, confident, and a gifted healer. She was also lovely, vivacious, and undeniably attractive. And that's why he wasn't comfortable around her. She made him think of things he couldn't have. Things he didn't deserve, like the soft touch of a lover's hand, or waking up with a warm, lush body nestled beside him.

"*Enough*," he told himself inwardly. That part of his life was over. With a grunt, he stretched, forcing himself to move as a way of pushing aside thoughts that served no purpose.

His shoulder popped and his spine cracked as he moved. "I'm getting old," he muttered.

An unexpected chuckle made him look up to find Sulat leaning against one side door just inside the space they called their reading nook. "Age has nothing to do with it. You've been sitting in that chair for the last four hours. You're not a cyborg, which means you need to move from time to time."

Sulat held his arms folded casually across his bare chest, and he had one leg crossed over the other at the ankle. The male's fair hair had strands of silver in it now, and the lines around his eyes deepened when he smiled, but his best friend still looked much the same as he had the first day they'd met... and beaten the hell out of each other.

Tariq waved off his friend's comment. "You do the same thing when you're in your lab. You get lost in what you're doing and it's like the rest of the universe vanishes from your awareness."

"That's true," Sulat admitted. "But at least I went out in public today."

"The practice arena barely counts." Tariq set down his tablet and took a closer look at his *anrik*. Several already-fading bruises marked his bare arms and torso.

"I hope you gave out as many strikes as you received. You're defending the family honor, after all."

"The family honor is intact. Though it wouldn't hurt you to come with me now and then. Some of the younger ones think you've retired from combat." Sulat lowered his voice. "You know, because you're too old."

"I'm the same age as you." The words were out before he could stop himself.

"So come with me next time and show the next generation they're not ready to take us on. I can't fend them all off on my own."

"Maybe I will." Tariq raised a hand. "*Maybe*."

"I'll accept that. For now. But while you were ignoring the world, you also missed a message from Vixi. She wants us to come over for dinner tonight."

"*Qarf*. I owe her an apology, then." He rose from his chair and took a moment to stretch his back, arms, and wings. "I assume you accepted for both of us?"

"Of course. When have either of us ever turned down a chance to spend time with our little whirlwind?"

"Never."

Sulat nodded. "I need to clean up and change. Then we can fly over to her place."

"I prefer to walk," he reminded his *anrik*.

"I know. But she's already worried about you. If we show up on foot..." he trailed off and lifted his wings in a shrug.

Sulat was right. Vixi didn't need to know he still avoided flying whenever possible. Every time he took to the air, memories of that final flight with Raenia consumed him.

"It's a short flight," Sulat said sympathetically.

"I'll manage."

"You always do."

They touched wrists before parting. The gesture was meant to remind them both that they were there for each other. Friends and brothers. Always.

That's what he needed to focus on now, his family. Vixi was wrong. He didn't need anyone else, especially not the attractive Dr. Clark. His interest in her had to be purely professional. Anything else would be a betrayal of Raenia's memory. And memories were all he had left.

∽

It was only a few minutes to make the flight to Vixi's residence. She'd chosen to live in one of the new structures on the far side of the river that flowed through the middle of the colony. At one time, the river had acted as a de facto border with the human cyborgs living on one side and the Vardarians on the other.

That wasn't the case anymore. The work of blending the various species into one community was still in progress, but the attacks on their home had brought the two main species together.

No. Tariq corrected himself. Not two species. Three. The cyborgs considered themselves separate from humans, even though they shared the same DNA.

Tariq distracted himself with musings about the colony's inhabitants and the changes he saw as they flew overhead. It helped to keep the darker thoughts at bay. If he could keep himself distracted, maybe he could return to the skies.

That thought was torn away by an unexpected downdraft that shoved them both toward the ground. It only lasted a moment and forced them less than three meters lower, but it unleashed a maelstrom of memories that swept him back to the moment of Raenia's death.

The skies had been clear when they'd set out together. They'd had no destination in mind and no plan other than to stretch their wings. Raenia loved to fly, and he loved to watch her wheel and soar. Always pushing herself higher and faster... until a sudden downdraft caught her and tossed her to the ground like an insect swatted by a giant hand.

Distracted by the past, Tariq nearly missed Vixi's rooftop and had to back wing hard to slow himself down. Even then, he landed hard and stumbled, his mind too tangled up in memories to pay attention to the here and now.

Sulat managed to get in front of him and caught hold

of his shoulders, stopping his momentum before he reached the edge.

Tariq steadied himself and straightened, but Sulat didn't let go. "Does it still bother you?"

"What do you think?" Of course, the memories still haunted him. "I'll never forget."

Sulat's grip tightened. "It's not about forgetting. But you can't let what happened affect you this way forever. You need to let it go."

Tariq's anger flared white-hot, and he had to fight the urge to shove his friend away. "Don't tell me how to live my life."

"That's the thing. It's not just your life. Vixi is worried about you, and so am I." Sulat's scales shimmered a brilliant silver as they tightened in anger. "Our daughter needs you to be present in her life. I want my *anrik* around, despite the fact he's a stubborn *bakaffa*."

They both laughed—more to break the tension than because of the joke—but it was enough. His anger faded and died like a flame denied oxygen. The confrontation turned into a brief embrace, and then it was done.

They took a moment to straighten out hair and clothing disheveled by the wind in companionable silence. There would be another conversation soon, but now wasn't the time. It annoyed him that Sulat was right. *Again.*

Damn the male for knowing him so well. He'd have to do better. Pay more attention to the family he had left.

Vixi's home fascinated Jody. Her residence was based on the same template, but there were differences in furnishing styles and the use of space Jody had never considered. The need for higher ceilings and wide doors was obvious enough given the Vardarian's larger size and wings, but as she looked around, it was obvious she'd need to rearrange some of her furniture. She'd set it up for a human home, and these were something different.

They were seated in a large, airy space in what Jody would call a conversation area with several comfortable options for seating gathered in a rough circle with a table in the center. The late afternoon sun came through the many windows, splashing down over the palette of cool pastels Vixi had decorated with.

"Do the new colonists receive any guidance on how to furnish and use the homes they'll receive once they graduate to full citizenship?" she asked Vixi.

"No. Why would they need that? They can furnish it however they like."

Even as she spoke, Vixi's brow furrowed in thought. "Except some of them have never had a private space of their own. Never mind an entire residence. *Veth*, we should have considered that."

Vixi cursed in Galactic Common as often as she did her own language. Study and time spent with the colonists on the journey here had given her more time to learn the language. For now, Jody had to rely on her translator, a bit of Vardarian tech she and Lores had been given shortly after their arrival. Tariq and Sulat had done the implantations, explaining each part of the procedure as they went. It was her first chance to see the two males in their roles as healers, and it had impressed her.

Since then, she'd hoped to work with them and learn more about Vardarian treatments and medicine, but so far that hadn't happened. They weren't even working out of the same med-clinic, which felt counter-productive. They had so much to learn from each other. Not to mention the imminent birth of the first Vardarian-human hybrid child. Reading and research could give her the facts, but she wanted to hear about their *experiences*, too. Vixi's invitation to dinner with her family had seemed like the perfect opportunity to talk.

"You and your team have done an amazing job. I only ask because now that I've seen your home, I see a few areas where I didn't grasp the purpose of the space." She gestured around them, indicating the three-dimensional artwork and furnishings laid out to create glide paths between the various areas.

Alcoves and smaller rooms were generally set against the outer walls, and many of them extruded past the wall to create more space.

Vixi nodded thoughtfully. "I had a similar experience while on Earth. Everything felt too closed in and cramped. It was difficult to find somewhere I could spread my wings, and flying..." she shook her head. "I've never been grounded for so long in my life."

"Being underground is difficult enough. But for you..." Jody raised her hands and sketched out a vague wing shape above her shoulders. "How did you manage?"

"I had to request rooms in the section reserved for

Torski visitors. Not that they have many, but there are rooms set aside for them."

The Torskis were the largest sentient species in known space. They towered over humans, and even the Vardarians seemed small compared to the heavy-gravity worlders.

Jody was about to ask more about Vixi's experiences on Earth—a place she'd never been—when the household AI interrupted.

"Visitors have arrived. Identities confirmed. Grant access?" The voice was the same as her own AI, genderless and pleasant, always sounding soothing no matter what message it conveyed.

"Allow access," Vixi instructed. That done, she gave Jody a sheepish smile. "I should probably warn you that my fathers don't know they're not my only guests for dinner."

Jody kept her expression neutral, but inwardly she winced. Did the two healers dislike her so much they had to be tricked into dining with her? What would happen when they saw her sitting here?

"That's going to be awkward. Should I leave?" she offered.

"No. You're my guest and I'm happy you're here." Vixi seemed to sense Jody's sudden discomfort and leaned over to place a hand on her arm. "I'm sorry. I should have said something earlier. I was enjoying our conversation and forgot."

Footsteps sounded on the stairs leading down from the rooftop, and Jody tensed.

"My fathers need to stop hiding away from the world.

You're their colleague, and I know they both admire you. We can, as you humans say, talk shop."

They admired her? That was news to Jody, but she knew Vixi well enough to trust her judgment. Especially when it came to her own parents.

Tariq arrived first, grinning broadly as he looked around for his daughter. The grin faltered and then flickered and died when he spotted Jody. "You have company, Vixi? Did Sulat get the wrong day?"

Sulat appeared a second later and reacted differently. "Hello, Dr. Clark. Pleasure to see you outside of work," he said and flashed Jody a friendly smile. At the same time, he subtly tapped Tariq on the back with one wing in what she suspected was the Vardarian version of an elbow to the ribs.

Tariq must have taken the hint because he gave her a polite nod. "Good evening, Dr. Clark."

Vixi popped up from her chair and hurried over to hug her fathers. "Hi, Dads. You're here on the right day. Did I forget to mention I had invited Jody, too?"

This gave Jody a chance to collect herself. The first thing she did was offer them both a friendly smile and a slight wave of acknowledgment. Then she watched as the family greeted each other with hugs and obvious affection.

Vixi took after Sulat in looks, though something about the way she moved reminded her more of Tariq. She wondered if Vixi was a blend of all three parents' genetic material, or if her mannerisms were a learned behavior. As far as Jody knew, both types of reproduction were common in their culture. Species purity was far more important than paternity.

The two males were undeniably attractive. Both had silver scales, but they were otherwise quite different. Sulat was warm, bright, and cheerful with fair hair touched with silver and a sunny smile. Tariq was darker, both in looks and manner. A few strands of gray showed in his hair, and his demeanor was darker and somehow more sultry...or maybe that was only her imagination. Stars knew she'd imagined an awful lot about them. They might be off limits in the real world, but within the confines of her imagination, there were no rules. Not that she'd ever admit that to anyone else.

Warmth and desire bloomed within her, heating her cheeks. She had to lower her head to hide her face, concerned her feelings might show in her expression. Not that she knew what she was feeling, exactly. Her nervousness over their unexpected arrival was all mixed up in the fluttery feelings of physical attraction and embarrassment at her reaction to them.

She needed to get her *fraxxing* head together and stop crushing on her colleagues.

Vixi sent her fathers to get comfortable while she checked on their meal.

"What's for dinner?" Sulat asked.

"*Natambe*," Vixi replied in her own language.

Jody's translator converted the word to *meat food*, which wasn't overly helpful. "My translator can't parse that word. All I know is that dinner smells delicious. What are we having?"

Sulat answered. "Skewered meat, usually *gharshtu*.

It's seasoned, roasted, and served with roasted tubers and vegetables."

To her surprise, Tariq joined the conversation. "And *tazin*. Can't forget that."

"*Tazin?*" Jody asked. Her translator only said it was a *chilled sauce*.

"It's delicious," Tariq said and then raised his voice. "Vixi, how do you describe it in Dr. Clark's language?"

"It's a creamy dip that counters some of the spices used on the meat," Vixi called back from the kitchen.

Jody noted that the acoustics of the place allowed voices to carry easily. Living alone, she hadn't noticed it before. As social as humans were, it was common for them to seek private spaces to relax. Vardarian homes were apparently designed to allow the residents to stay connected.

"I can't wait to try it. My food processor was programmed for mostly human meals, and I haven't had much time to update the recipe selections."

"Really? I can send you some of my favorites," Vixi called out again. "I'm no chef, but I love good food. In fact, that's something else we should do for the others as they move into the main colony. Give them a selection of meals to try along with some of the standard ones they get now."

"That's a good idea," Sulat agreed.

Tariq nodded. "While you're at it, could you send those recipes to us, too? Sulat's made the same thing three times this week."

"No, I reheated and served you the same food three days in a row because you barely touched it every time, and I was trying to make a point." Sulat made a face. "Obviously I failed."

"You served me food that was three days old?" Tariq demanded.

"You didn't eat it, so I don't see the problem."

Vixi stepped into view. She still held a pair of tongs in one hand and gestured with them as she spoke. "Dad, you promised me you'd eat more."

She pointed the tongs at Sulat next. "Stop provoking him. I know you didn't serve him the same food three days in a row. You made the same thing three times. Didn't you?"

Sulat laughed and raised his hands. "You're right. It was the same thing made fresh each night."

"I've been distracted," Tariq admitted.

"That's one word for it," Sulat teased.

Tariq's lips twitched into a brief smile. "I get to things, eventually."

Vixi snickered. "Does that mean you've finally finished unpacking? I mean, we've only been here a year or so."

"Don't sass your elders," Tariq scolded, his words at odds with his light, laughing tone.

"Or do we need to bring up certain moments from your past to entertain Dr. Clark while we wait for dinner?"

Jody laughed and tried to sound casual as she made the request she'd been trying to voice for weeks. "Please call me Jody. We're not at work right now. There's no need to be formal. And I would love to hear some of

Vixi's childhood stories. I can trade you for some of my son's."

"You have a son?" Sulat asked. "I didn't realize. He didn't come with you to Haven?"

"Jacob is too old to follow his mother around anymore. He joined the AIF last year and is leading his own life now." She chuckled softly and lowered her voice to a conspirator's whisper. "Which means he isn't around to complain when I tell his most embarrassing stories."

"It's one of the best parts of being a parent. Right, Riq?" Sulat joked.

"Revenge," Tariq agreed with a wicked smile.

She liked this unguarded and informal version of Tariq. Some of Jody's concerns faded as the three of them exchanged stories about their children. Vixi returned with drinks and joined in, attempting to defend herself.

"How was I supposed to know it was one of your experiments? It was in our kitchen and I was thirsty." She exclaimed at one point.

Tariq pointed at his *anrik* and laughed harder. "Raenia was furious when she found out you'd stored that stuff in the house. I thought she might kill you."

"You're the one who told her what happened!" Sulat retorted, laughing almost as hard as Tariq. "I'd already bribed our little whirlwind into keeping it a secret, and you ruined it."

"And you told mom about our deal, too." Vixi pouted. "I lost out on a bunch of candy and games Dad promised to buy me."

Jody stayed quiet and watched the interaction. It was the first time any of them had brought up Vixi's mother.

Chapter 3

Tariq quieted, one hand straying to the arm band on his left biceps. The *harani* was identical to the one Sulat wore. It showed their status as mated males, though the sky-blue color showed they were in mourning for their mate.

Sulat let the mention of his lost mate slip past without comment, choosing to continue teasing Vixi instead. "I still don't understand what made you want to drink it. As I recall, the stuff was a vile shade of green and stank. No sane being would ever consider consuming that. You never told me why you did it."

Vixi's lips twisted in an expression Jody hadn't seen before, and the young female flashed her fangs at her father. "It looked like the potion Kashtar drank when she turned herself into a..." she glanced at Jody. "Superhero. Is that the phrase?"

"You drank your dad's experiment because you wanted special powers?" Jody didn't even try to keep the amusement out of her voice. "Oh, you really must meet Jake one day. He broke his wrist during an attempt to see if he could fly."

Vixi looked puzzled. "I thought that wasn't a human ability?"

"It isn't, but that doesn't stop some children from trying. They see vids and hear stories about such things and..." Jody shook her head. "He was more upset to discover he was an ordinary human than he was about his injury."

Tariq glanced at his daughter with a bemused smile. "For children, everything is an adventure. For their parents, it's one set of worries after another."

Vixi rolled her eyes, a very human expression she must have picked up from the colonists. "Dad, I'm an adult now. You can stop worrying."

All three of them chimed in at the same time with variations of the same statement. "We never stop worrying."

It was a moment of camaraderie, one she hoped would bring them closer together as friends. It was all she could hope for. Anything else was just fodder for her late-night fantasies.

4

Sulat didn't want the evening to end. He always enjoyed spending time with Vixi, but tonight was special. Jody added a new dynamic to their normally quiet family gatherings. Her infectious laughter was contagious, and her interest in learning more about Vardarian customs and attitudes carried the conversation through their meal and beyond.

Why had he avoided getting to know her better until now? Vixi's machinations had surprised them both on arrival, but now he was happy she'd intervened, even if she'd tricked them into it. When Tariq had used their internal comm line to demand what she was up to, their little whirlwind had smiled sweetly and replied that if they wouldn't help themselves, she'd have to do it for them.

Apparently, she was right.

"Does anyone need a snack? Dinner was hours ago," Vixi said.

"I'd love to stay and try more of your cooking, but I

think it's time I went home." Jody smiled and pointed to herself. "Unlike all of you, I don't have medi-bots or nanotech to help me stay awake."

Qarf. He'd forgotten about that. As a new arrival, Jody wouldn't be offered the enhancements immediately. All new human colonists had to pass the training and be accepted as full citizens before that happened. Accepting the treatment also meant abiding by the rule set by the humans' governing body. They had to stay on the planet for the rest of their lives.

Sulat didn't understand the restriction. Vardarians were free to come and go as they pleased. Only the humans and cyborgs were subject to that rule, and there were reports the human military was giving the tech to some of their soldiers.

The winds of change had already scattered the knowledge of the nanotech across the sector. There was no stopping it, but the rule was still in place—at least for now. A growing number of beings wanted it struck down, and he agreed with them.

"Of course. I should have considered that," Vixi said, slightly chagrined. "Shall I call for a transport?"

"No transport needed. I'll walk. It's a lovely night," Jody said and rose to her feet.

Once again, he was reminded that her personality was bigger than her physical body, at least to him. Vixi had informed him that Jody was tall for a human female, but to him, she seemed small.

Tariq stood as well. "We will escort you home, Jody."

The declaration caught him off guard. Not that he

was opposed to the idea, but it wasn't what he'd expected from his *anrik*.

"It would be our honor," Sulat said.

"I'll be fine. Haven is the safest place I've lived in over ten years." Jody raised a hand to wave off their offer but then hesitated. "But I wouldn't mind having company, though. I haven't had much time to learn the layout of this place. I confess I've gotten lost more than once."

Vixi's face scrunched up with in confusion. "How could that happen? Your comm unit has a map function. Doesn't it?"

"It does. But if I relied on tech to accomplish everything, I wouldn't learn much. Would I?"

It was an interesting question. Like the rest of his species, Sulat had been born with a body full of nanotech. As an adult, he now had additional tech implanted—including a subdermal comm unit and a translation matrix. Flying was the only time he spent away from most of the day-to-day technology that enhanced his life in a thousand ways.

"Does this mean you don't intend to accept the nanotech treatment if it's offered to you?" Tariq asked.

"I don't know. As much as I am enjoying this place, it's not my home. Not yet, anyway. Long life and perfect health are wonderful benefits, but it comes with restrictions I'm not sure I could accept. My son is out there." She gestured toward the ceiling and the sky beyond. "What if he needs me and I can't help him because I'm trapped here?"

Sulat turned to look at Vixi. If his child was in

trouble, he'd break every law in the galaxy to reach her. Consequences be damned. No doubt Jody would do the same. But how? Security measures were so tight they couldn't even send one of the senior human colonists back to Earth to talk about her experiences and help ease the new recruits' worries before and during the voyage back.

Tariq looked thunderous as the thought of being kept away from their daughter sank in. "That law is ridiculous and should be struck down. Everyone should have the right to travel wherever and whenever they wish."

"I agree." Jody raised and lowered her shoulders in what he had learned was their version of a dismissive shrug. "But for now, it stands. Besides, my situation is unique. I'm not a colonist. I'm on a three-year employment contract. The treatment would be available if I decided to stay."

"I hope you decide to stay with us." The words were out before he noticed his mouth moving. "I mean, stay here in Haven." Sulat winced at his own awkwardness.

Jody gifted him with a smile that warmed him to his soul. "We'll see what the future holds. For now, I'm only concerned about tomorrow. I've got a new patient to see. One of yours, in fact. Cameron Allen."

"He finally took our recommendation to come and speak to you?" Tariq asked.

"Took him long enough," Sulat grumbled.

Allen was the only full-blooded human male in the colony. He enjoyed his status immensely, especially when it came to unmated females, who considered him a new delicacy to be sampled. Despite his easygoing demeanor, the male had suffered abuse several times in his past and had various scars and injuries his recently gained medi-bots were unable to address.

"Don't let him get flirty," Vixi chimed in. "He thinks he's more charming than he actually is."

Sulat stiffened, but Tariq spoke first. "He flirted with you?"

Jody burst out laughing, her gray eyes sparkling with mirth. "Now you've done it. He better come to me for all future treatments, or these two are likely to prescribe him a fatherly warning about putting the moves on their little girl."

"Witnessed," Tariq muttered, his expression stormy.

Vixi scowled. "Not you, too, Jody. I'm over thirty years old by human standards. I haven't been *little* for decades."

"But you will always be our little whirlwind," Sulat said.

"And with that, I will bid all of you good night." Vixi rose and used her hands and her wings to gesture toward the stairs leading down to street level.

Jody turned toward the other female and gave her a hug. "Dinner was wonderful. Thank you for the invitation. I had a lovely time. We'll have to organize a date so I can return the favor and host you and your fathers over for dinner."

Vixi beamed. "I'd like that. We'd love to come to your home. Perhaps next week?"

"That works. I can check with your fathers on the way home and find an evening that works for everyone."

Jody glanced over at the two males. "If that's alright with you?"

"We'll sort out the details during our walk," Sulat said before Tariq could open his mouth and blast the idea out of the sky. Not that he was certain that would happen. His *anrik's* thoughts had been turbulent and hard to read for weeks now. Tonight, he was more like himself, but Sulat would assume nothing until they'd had time to talk privately. He wanted to know Jody better. *Much better*. But that couldn't happen without Tariq. Whatever happened, they'd make this decision the way they made all others—together.

∽

The evening had filled Jody's soul as well as her stomach. It had been too long since she'd spent a relaxed evening with good company. Lores didn't count. They had been friends so long they'd heard all of each other's stories. Tonight was different, like her new life had finally started.

She appreciated the chance to get to know Sulat and Tariq better, despite the way Vixi had ambushed the three of them. It wasn't the smoothest of beginnings—but she had to admit, it worked.

The three of them strolled through the colony. Tariq walked to her left and Sulat on her right. The big males both altered their stride to match hers, though she did her best to walk briskly so they didn't have to slow down too much.

They pointed out various shops and made a few

recommendations on where to find some of the household items she wanted to acquire. While her new home came with basic furnishings, she wanted to add her own touches, including some of the elements she'd seen tonight.

When they reached the midpoint of the walk, Sulat shifted his wings in a way she'd learned was the Vardarian equivalent of clearing one's throat before speaking.

She turned her head in his direction but then had to move quickly to look at Tariq when he spoke first.

"Now we are alone I wanted to say that you do not have to include me or Sulat in your invitation to dinner. That would leave you free to enjoy an evening with Vixi without us."

Sulat made a noise somewhere between a growl and a huff of annoyance. "Do not speak for me, Riq. We may not be of the same mind."

Tariq stopped and stared at his *anrik*. Neither of them spoke aloud, but Jody saw the subtle movements of their jaw and lips and knew they were conversing via their internal comms.

Their conversation ended quickly enough things didn't get overly awkward, but it still deflated some of her buoyant mood.

"I accept your invitation for dinner," Sulat's declaration broke the silence.

"As do I," Tariq said. "I only wished to ensure you didn't feel pressured. Vixi's enthusiasm can sometimes place others in difficult positions."

Jody laughed and nodded. "You mean like inviting

the three of us to dinner and not mentioning to any of us that there would be other guests?"

Tariq's lips twitched in amusement. "Yes. Exactly like that."

Jody once again marveled at the way the male's smile transformed his appearance. It made him so much more approachable—and appealing.

"I would like to have you *all* over for dinner and conversation. We are colleagues, and that means we should know each other better so we can work as a team."

Both males nodded in agreement, and Jody felt a tingle of anticipation at the idea of seeing them both again. *Only as friends*, she reminded herself. Even so, this was an important step in their relationship. Their *professional* relationship.

They set off again, only to stop suddenly when her comm uttered several strident chirps. *Veth*. That specific pattern meant there was a situation with a special patient —Phaedra, the very pregnant princess.

In the time it took her to retrieve her comm unit and call up the message, both Sulat and Tariq had unfurled their wings and moved into the street, clearly preparing to take to the air.

"With me, Jody!" Sulat pointed to a spot directly in front of him.

The command in his voice was so compelling she took several steps toward him before she even realized what she'd done. She hadn't read the *fraxxing* message yet. How could they know more than she did?

"Why? What's happened?" she demanded.

Chapter 4

Tariq gestured her forward and pitched his voice low. "It's begun."

Fraxx. The princess was in labor? "It's too soon," she murmured, certain they'd hear her. Vardarian senses were all more acute than humans.

"We estimated she had at least ten to fifteen days left," Sulat said, matching their low tones.

That was one of the challenges they faced with Phaedra. She was the first human female to become pregnant with a Vardarian child. That left them with a measure of uncertainty about gestation time and what the delivery would look like.

To complicate matters further, the parents had chosen not to alter the child's DNA. Not only did this go against societal norms, but it added more unknowns to the whole process. Jody agreed with their decision, but it didn't make her job any easier.

"You two should go ahead. I'll call for a vehicle and meet you there." She didn't mention their destination. The princess was in hiding until her child was born. The decision not to alter the baby's DNA had triggered a backlash of judgment and discontent from the more xenophobic elements of Vardarian society, including some here in Haven.

Sulat shook his head and slashed the air with his hand. "That will take too long. I'll carry you."

"Carry me?" She pointed toward the sky. "Up there?"

"Yes. Now come here." Sulat pointed in front of him again.

Was there a hint of heat in his eyes when he said it?

She couldn't be certain, but her pulse leaped and a tingle of anticipation sizzled through her veins at the thought, followed immediately by a flash of guilt. Phaedra should be her focus right now. She was a doctor and could not let herself be distracted by fantasies and infatuation.

"Go with Sulat. I will follow as quickly as I can."

Follow? Why did Tariq think he'd fall behind when Sulat was the one burdened by her weight? She left the question unasked but made a mental note to ask about it another time.

Sulat caught her hands in his and drew them up to his shoulders. "Hold on like this," he said.

She tangled her fingers in the embroidered expanse of fabric that formed the collar of his tunic and tightened her grip. Every muscle in her body tensed as adrenaline flooded her system. "Ready."

His lips lifted in a brief smile that made her heart race and her entire body tingle. "No, you're not. Close your eyes and take a long, slow breath. This will be easier if you relax and trust me to take control."

She intended to nod and stay quiet, but her *fraxxing* mouth didn't get the memo. "Did you just ask me to submit to you?"

The words were out before she could stop herself. Stars-fury, she shouldn't have had that last glass of liquor at dinner. So much for acting like a professional.

Jody braced for Sulat's reaction. Would he be shocked? Angry? Outraged? Or all of the above? Probably the last one, she decided as she stared up at the big male while inwardly praying the ground would open up and swallow her.

Chapter 4

For several seconds he stared at her, his expression an unreadable mask. Then he smiled so broadly she could see his fangs. She was so surprised she almost missed the way his scales tightened, making his skin's color change to a brighter gold that seemed to glow in the soft light of the streetlamps.

His green eyes burned with a desire so intense she forgot to breathe. "Trust comes before submission, little *zurya*. But if that is your desire..." he bowed his head to brush the gentlest of kisses across her lips.

Tariq uttered a low snarl. "Enough of that. We have a patient to attend."

Jody's stomach twisted, and she jerked her head away from Sulat's touch, her cheeks heating with embarrassment. "You two fly. I'll call a ride."

"No. You come with me, Jody." Then he turned to bare his fangs at his *anrik*. "Some of us want more from life than endless work and solitude, Riq. You owe Jody an apology for that outburst."

Tariq turned his back to them and launched himself into the air without another word.

Fraxx. What had she done?

"Ignore him. He is as stubborn as a *mogat* with a migraine. He will regret what he said soon enough. Then you will have your apology."

"He has nothing to apologize for. He's right. Our patient is our priority." She sighed. "I'm embarrassed. Let's pretend this never happened."

"No," he declared, "I will not forget this." He touched one hand to his chest and then raised it in a gesture like he was offering something to the sky. "I swear by the breath in my lungs that you have nothing to be embarrassed about."

Jody was stunned. The vow he'd given her was steeped in tradition and considered unbreakable. She answered the best she could, not sure if any formal response was required. "*Atarflorinti*," she said, acknowledging his statement.

"Now we can go. Don't worry, *zurya*. We'll arrive first despite the delay."

Zurya. That was the second time he'd called her that. It meant blossom in his language. Despite everything that had just happened, the endearment delighted her. *Veth*, she needed to have her head examined.

"How can we catch up now?" she asked.

He didn't answer. Instead, he pulled her in close and then swept her up into his arms, cradling her against the hard planes of his chest. She renewed her grip on his collar and shut her eyes, willing herself to relax.

She expected him to lunge into the air, wings beating hard to accommodate her extra weight. Instead, he surged upward almost effortlessly.

Heart racing, she couldn't resist peeking down. She expected them to still be close to the ground. They weren't. Her heart nearly stopped and her stomach dropped when all she could see of the colony were rooftops and roadways.

She squeaked and buried her head in the crook of his neck. Her fingers gripped tighter, but she managed not to freeze up. She had to trust him. She *did* trust him. But that trust was all tangled up with a host of other emotions she didn't have time to address right now.

Chapter 4

Think of this as a team building exercise, she told herself. Yeah, right. This had nothing to do with teamwork or professional development.

They had a patient to tend to and a job to do. She had to stay focused, which was easier said than done when Sulat's strong arms held her close and every breath she took carried the warm scent of him deep into her lungs.

5

Focusing on his irritation let Tariq stay clear of the dark thoughts that haunted him when he took to the air. Instead of regrets and grief, he indulged in a mental rant against his blood-bonded brother.

What the *qarf* was Sulat thinking? Why would he do that without talking things through first? If he needed release, they could purchase a pleasure bot. He'd considered that option more than once. But this... a human female? One they worked with? It was a terrible idea...especially since Jody's warm laugh and soft curves called to him, tempting him to think of things he had no right to have. Raenia was gone. The hole she left in his heart could never be filled. Any attempt to replace her was a betrayal of what they'd had with their *mahaya*, their one true mate.

Anger fueled his urgent flight to the palace, but even so, he had lost some of the strength in his wings. If he didn't start flying more, they'd continue to weaken. Given the heavier gravity of this world, he might eventually lose the ability to fly completely. The thought didn't bother him as much as he expected, and he wasn't sure what to think about that. Right now, he wasn't sure what the *fraxx* to think about anything.

When Sulat and Jody flew past him, it fueled another surge of irritation, but this one lacked the raw edges of the first bout. It was time to turn his attention to the needs of his patient. Phaedra was the first human he'd ever treated. She was also the reason Dr. Clark was here at all.

His *anrik* had already landed and stood speaking to one of the palace guards by the time Tariq arrived. He attempted to land perfectly, not wanting a repeat of his earlier failure. While Haven was far more relaxed and accepting than many parts of the Vardarian empire, appearances still mattered, and perception was important, especially when in and around the palace.

He was still drawing in his wings and straightening his clothing when he caught part of the conversation between the guard and Sulat.

"I'm sorry, Healer Vana. The rules are clear. No one may enter the palace through these doors. You need to fly to the front gate and present yourself to the guards there."

Sulat's voice was edged with frustration. "You're not listening." He gestured to himself, then Jody, and then to Tariq. "We are here at the prince's personal request. He instructed us to land here. Unless Guard Captain Doni has more authority than the prince himself, we will be entering the palace through *this* door."

The guard stiffened, his scales tightening. "I have my orders."

Chapter 5

Sulat crossed his arms and glowered at the younger male. "And we have ours."

Tariq opened his mouth to add his voice to Sulat's, but Jody spoke first.

"Guardsman, what is your name?" she demanded in a voice like a velvet-covered blade. He'd never heard her speak that way before, soft, but oh-so dangerous.

It intrigued him.

"I am Guardsman Ashik." The guard looked down at Jody with obvious interest. His wings rose behind him as he flexed the muscles of his upper torso. "You are Dr. Clark. Yes? The unclaimed human female?"

Tariq couldn't believe it. Was the guard attempting to flirt with Jody? She was with *them,* and they were standing right here. Jealousy surged through him, both unexpected and unfamiliar. How many years had it been since he'd felt this way? Decades at least. Learning to live with and love the same female hadn't always been easy, but he and Sulat had found their way through it.

He growled low in his throat, the sound blending with Sulat's snarl.

Without looking at either of them, Jody shifted position so she stood between them and the guardsman. Then she straightened to her full height, placed her hands on her hips, and shocked them all by barking out orders in passable Vardarian.

"You will let us pass, Guardsman Ashik. Now. Or do you wish me to inform the prince that we were delayed because you did not understand the chain of command? Move aside and let us do our job." Jody lifted one hand

and made a shooing gesture that reminded him of a mother dealing with a difficult child.

The guard moved aside, his expression sullen. That was no way for a royal guardsman to behave. Who was this male? Tariq had no idea, but he made a note to find out. No one should interfere with his ability to access the prince or his family. Too much was at stake.

He traded looks with Sulat, the two of them clearly of the same opinion. Jody pressed on, walking past the guard and into the palace without looking back.

He hurried to follow her with Sulat falling in beside him.

"*She has hidden depths.*" He sent the message to Sulat via their internal link.

"*Indeed. And I desire to explore all of them. The question is, are you interested in joining me? If so, you should stop being such a* bakaffa. *Winds and tides, you should stop acting that way even if you're not interested. She is a colleague worthy of our respect.*"

Tariq almost snorted aloud. "*Respect is not what you were showing her back there in the street. And this is not the time or place to discuss your sudden obsession with human females.*" Even as he said it, he knew he wasn't being fair.

"*Not all human females.*" Sulat flicked a finger toward Jody, who was now only a few steps ahead. "*Just one.*"

Anger threatened to spill over again, but this time, he kept it in check. He considered his next words carefully, weighing them for several long seconds. In the end, he kept it brief. *"For me, there can be no one else. Not now, not ever. If you wish to pursue her, you will do so alone."*

Sulat dropped his head quickly, but not fast enough to hide the hard look on his face. Then he lengthened his stride to catch up with the human doctor, leaving Tariq alone.

He found himself loath to join them. Instead, he lagged behind as he did his best to ignore the pang of regret that grew stronger as the distance increased. He'd meant what he said. He would be alone for the rest of his life. Raenia was the female he'd been fated to love. No one could replace her. So why did it feel like he was making a mistake?

6

Jody's thoughts tumbled around the inside of her head, all tangled up with each other. Vixi's ploy to bring the three of them together had blown up like a supernova. Instead of building trust and connections, she'd driven a wedge between Sulat and Tariq. Worse, her interest in them was now out in the open, despite all her attempts to hide it.

She'd assumed neither of them would be interested. Re'veth, had she been wrong there. Well, half wrong at least. Sulat was certainly interested. Tariq clearly wasn't, and that was a problem. This was her fault. She shouldn't have had anything to drink. She shouldn't have agreed to walk with them. She should have left the moment they arrived and Vixi confessed her plans.

"If wishes were sunshine, we'd always have light," she murmured to herself. It was one of her father's favorite sayings, and she'd said it to Jake many times when he was a boy. He liked it as little as she had when she was his age, but it was as true now as it had been back then.

"I have never heard that expression before." Sulat's deep voice caught her by surprise and she flinched.

He took her by the arm to steady her, the strength in his hand tempting her to lean into him even more.

"It's something my father used to say to me. I didn't even realize I'd said it aloud." She made an airy, dismissive gesture with her free hand.

"You did. And now I want to know what you were wishing for."

"I wasn't. Well, not really. I was just sorry about how this evening ended." She noticed he hadn't let go of her arm yet and gently withdrew it from his hand.

His green eyes caught hers and held her. "I do not regret any part of this evening, save for the way my *anrik* behaved. I need to speak with him, and then I will explain things to you."

She shook her head. "You don't have to do that. I understand. The female you were fated to love joined your ancestors far too soon. That changed your lives in profound and permanent ways. I have some idea how that feels, Sulat."

Her divorce wasn't the same as the loss Sulat and Tariq had suffered, but it was the only point of reference she had.

He nodded but said nothing else as they approached the door to the prince's private wing.

Two more guards stood on either side of the double door. It looked like ornately carved wood, but Jody had learned that it was actually made of metal plates so thick they could withstand significant force without buckling.

That information had arisen during her first tour of

the palace. When she asked why such measures were necessary, Phaedra had gone uncharacteristically quiet for several long seconds before answering, "Because not everyone agrees with what we are trying to create here. Tyran and Braxon left the empire for good reason, and so did many of those who joined the diaspora."

"Many, but not all?" she'd asked.

"Not from our perspective. Some are spies and troublemakers deliberately sent here. Mostly they report to the empress or one of the various factions that makes up her court. We were prepared for them, but others here want this colony to fail."

"Like the *Liq'za*? The ones who believe in racial and cultural purity?"

Phaedra had gathered her hands protectively over her rounded stomach and nodded. "Exactly."

Now, Jody needed to get past the guards and the same door to get to their patient. Everything about the two in her way, both in stance and expression, told her that would not be easy.

"Good evening. We are the healers the prince requested," she said.

One of the guards, a female, unfurled her wings in a blocking gesture and gave Jody a visual once-over before answering. "You did not register at the gate as you were instructed."

"Because the prince asked us to make our way here as quickly as possible."

Instead of answering her, the female turned to Sulat. "You and Healer A'Nir are known to me. Send the human back to register the three of you, and I will permit the two of you inside to attend to the prince."

Jody hadn't intended to push back, but the words that came out of her mouth were not the ones she'd planned on. "The human has a name. I am Doctor Clark, and I am also one of the prince's healers."

She reactivated her filters before anything else slipped out, and her next words were more in line with her original plan. "Please let us pass. The prince is waiting."

Again, the female guard ignored her to speak to Sulat, though this time she included the newly arrived Tariq in her address. "The prince is so ill he requires three healers? Why was I not informed?"

"The door slid open at that moment, revealing an agitated Prince Tyran standing on the other side. "You were not informed because this was supposed to be a discreet visit, Captain Doni."

The female immediately spun to face Tyran and saluted. "My apologies, Highness. Your healers were told they could pass."

Tyran's wings shifted. "That's not what I heard. Or did you forget this door is monitored as well as guarded? Dr. Clark, Healers A'Nir and Vana, thank you for coming so quickly. This way."

He turned and walked away from the guards without another word.

All three of them followed, none daring to break the silence until the door was once again sealed behind them.

"What in the six winds of Scera was that about?" Tariq asked.

"Power," Tyran spoke without looking back. "The games of court have started in earnest, and so far, I have not been able to stamp them out. Braxon wants to banish anyone who tries to play these foolish games. I'm starting to think he's right."

They walked in silence again, aware that even inside the prince's private space, it wasn't safe to speak about some matters. It wasn't until they reached his personal chambers, where no one but his most trusted servants had access, that they could talk without risk.

"What are her symptoms?" Tariq asked, his tone warm yet professional.

"She's in labor!" the mask of leadership fell away and Jody looked at a male racked with worry for his love and their unborn child.

"Are you sure?" Sulat asked.

"Of course we're not sure! But she's in pain and her stomach moves in the strangest ways."

Jody waited for one of the others to reassure Tyran, but no one spoke, not even to ask more questions. Instead, all of them looked at her for answers. "How much pain is she in? Is it coming at regular intervals?" she asked.

"She says it's uncomfortable, but she also said that when her cranial implants conflicted with a Vardarian translator and the headaches caused her to pass out." Tyran looked equally frustrated and adoring for a moment. "As you can imagine, we do not trust her to admit when she is in pain."

"Understandable." Jody nodded and then prompted him to answer her second question. "Is there a rhythm to these cramps?"

"I..." he scowled, suddenly looking much younger. "I don't know."

To her surprise, Tariq walked over and set a hand on the prince's shoulder, his expression one of compassion and understanding she'd never seen him wear before. "Your *mahaya* will be fine. We're here, and we'll work together to take care of her." He turned his gaze to her, and she basked in the unexpected warmth in his eyes. "You have the best team of healers on the planet."

Team of healers. Did he really think of her that way, or was this all a show for Tyran's benefit? She cast the unkind thought aside the moment it popped into her mind. For this moment, at least, that's how he saw them. Saw *her*. As one of the team.

Maybe this evening wasn't a total disaster after all.

"I know, but this is..." the prince grimaced with worry before mustering a smile. "I am grateful you are here, Dr. Clark. You came highly recommended, and I know you already have Phaedra's trust. Come, I will take you to her."

"Is it safe to do that?" With the threats against Phaedra and her baby, the princess had been in hiding for as long as Jody had been on the planet. Most of their appointments were done by video conferencing while a medical bot ran the tests and examinations. Not even Rae had access to the royal consort. The construct had been hacked once already, nearly killing someone. They couldn't risk it.

Jody had only seen Phaedra a few times in person, and that had involved a great deal of secrecy, undisclosed locations, and the occasional use of untraceable shuttles.

"Quite safe." The prince walked over to an alcove and twisted the top, or maybe it was the head of an abstract sculpture.

Across the room, another alcove with a matching statue rotated, leaving a narrow opening. "This way."

From the expressions on her companions' faces, neither of them was aware of the secret door either.

"Where are we going? Another shuttle port?" Sulat asked.

"Nothing so complicated this time." Tyran passed through the door and gestured for them to follow, his motions more urgent now.

Once they were all in the narrow but brightly lit corridor, Tyran tapped a keypad and the door closed behind them. "You see, Phaedra has returned to the palace."

Tariq chuckled. "I wondered how you could stay away from your *mahaya* for so long. It isn't in our nature, especially when they are carrying our offspring. I found it difficult to let Raenia out of my sight for more than a few minutes."

"And it infuriated her," Sulat added.

Sulat lifted both wings before resetting them against his back. "I was not the only one who hovered. As I recall, she threatened to throw us both out of our bed if we didn't give her more space."

The friendly banter between the two healers was intended to ease the prince's worries or at least distract him for a time. It seemed to work.

Tyran's smile warmed. "I had to change the codes for the door to ensure she didn't sneak out one night while

Braxon and I slept. Our little warrior resents the need to stay hidden."

This last statement came as they reached the end of the corridor and stepped through an open archway. Beyond it was a perfect replica of the quarters they'd seen upstairs, complete with windows that were actually framed vid-screens with select views of the palace grounds. Jody could only see only two differences. The first was a tall, golden-skinned male on the far side of the room. The other was a pink-haired, heavily pregnant princess wearing a flowing robe as black as the scowl on her face.

"You changed the *fraxxing* code because you're keeping me a prisoner!" she said.

"We're keeping you safe," the prince and his *anrik* said at the same time in tones that made it clear they'd had this conversation many times before.

"Safe is boring! Next time, you can stay down here and I'll deal with the idiots at court."

Braxon folded his arms. "I'm stuck down here too, Phae."

Phaedra glowered at him. "How could I forget? You're always there. Just a few meters away, watching me like I'm made of crystal and could shatter at any second."

Her rant was cut off as her face twisted into a grimace and one hand went to her belly. "Also, if this is labor, I would like a pain-blocker please. If it's not labor, can you make it stop?"

Phaedra got to her feet without too much trouble. When Tyran moved to help, she held up one hand to him and the other toward Braxon. "Don't either of you move.

Do not come near me. No hovering, no smothering. In fact, do not even breathe in my direction."

"But," the prince protested.

"No buts!"

Tariq and Sulat moved as if they had rehearsed this moment, one of them gesturing for the males to follow him while the other approached Phaedra. "What do you need right now?" Tariq asked her.

"Answers." Phaedra managed a weak smile. "And the new door code, if you have it."

"I don't, but as your healer, I must consider your mental as well as your physical wellbeing. Make a list of things you'd like to have brought down here, and we'll see that it happens. Perhaps a small garden could be created? Or a sim-projector?"

Phaedra's eyes lit up. "Yes to both. I got used to breathing natural air and smelling green, growing things. I miss it. And while holograms aren't a real escape, they'd beat being bored as hell day after day."

As much as Jody wanted to keep watching the interaction between healer and patient, she needed to get to work. While the two of them talked, she found the nearest data terminal and tapped in her security code. It prompted her to scan her palm, her retina, and even provide a breath sample before finally granting her access to Phaedra's medical files.

What she saw confirmed her suspicions, though she wanted to do a physical examination to be sure. Smiling with relief, she returned to their patient, who was now visibly calmer and seated once again. Tariq had done a wonderful job soothing the soon-to-be mother.

"Phaedra, are you still feeling the same sensations now? If so, are they stronger or weaker than before?"

"They're still happening, but I think they're weaker now." Phaedra looked up at her hopefully. "Does that mean I'm not in labor?"

"I believe so." She glanced over at Tariq. "Do you know where the med-bay is? I need a hand scanner to confirm things."

"Brax, baby, we need the hand scanner," Phaedra called out before anyone could say another word. "If you promise not to fuss at me, you can stay after you bring it."

Braxon, Tyran, and Sulat all returned together, carrying the scanner and several other useful items. Armed with everything she needed, it was only a matter of minutes to perform the scans while gathering more information from Phaedra.

When she was confident of her diagnosis, Jody offered Phaedra a reassuring smile. "I can confirm that you're not in labor. You and the baby are healthy and strong, but you still have a while to wait before you get to meet your daughter."

The only beings on the planet who knew the sex of the child were currently in this room, and mentioning it brought smiles to everyone's faces.

Everyone one but Braxon. He dropped into a crouch at Phaedra's side, his eyes on her stomach. "Then what's wrong? Why is she in pain?"

Jody stepped back so she could address them all at once, though she directed her words to her patient. "Phaedra, your body is preparing for labor. What you're feeling is quite normal."

"Normal!" Tyran moved to stand behind his *mahaya* and placed his hands on her shoulders. Then he glowered at Jody. "It's distressing her. Make it stop."

Jody held up a placating hand, giving herself a brief window of time to pick her next words. Her professional side understood the situation and how to handle it. Deep in her heart, she felt a bittersweet rush of emotions, happiness and joy for Phaedra that she had such loving and supportive mates and a familiar pang of sadness that her own husband had prioritized his career over her and his only son. He hadn't even been around for most of her pregnancy because he'd volunteered to be deployed on a mission so secret, she learned nothing about it.

"The only way to make the practice contractions stop is for Phaedra to go into labor for real. That will happen in due time. I promise you all that this is quite normal for human pregnancy. I've checked the scans and everything is fine. Phaedra and the baby are healthy."

Tariq joined the conversation. "I am prescribing a holo-sim pod to be installed as well."

Tyran and Braxon nodded, the gestures perfectly in synch.

"Of course!" Braxon said.

"Whatever our little warrior needs," Tyran agreed.

Phaedra's brow furrowed, but her lips curved up in a tiny smile at the same time. "What your *mahaya* needs is for her mates to stop treating her like she's a tiskalian ice orchid. I won't shatter in a stiff breeze for *fraxx's* sake."

Sulat and Tariq shared a look that made both of them chuckle. Then Sulat spoke, "As healers, our advice is to be patient with the process."

Tariq nodded and then added, "And as two males who have been through this situation ourselves, our advice is to listen to your *mahaya*. She will let you know what she needs. Hovering over her like a broody *gharshtu* isn't healthy..." He looked at the prince and then Braxon. "For the two of you. Pregnant females can be dangerous when irked."

"But..." Tyran spoke first.

"She needs us," Braxon finished.

Phaedra huffed out a frustrated breath. "I'm dangerous when irked. Remember? Listen to the healers. They are wise."

The princess winked at Jody. "If they don't behave, could you leave a few vials of tranquilizer around? You know—for my mental health?"

"I'll consider it." She grinned and winked back. "But for now, my instructions are for you to get some rest. I am also prescribing a soothing shower and a foot rub. By the time you finish the first two, your body should have ended the practice session, and you'll be ready to sleep."

"I'll take care of her," Braxon stated with solemn intent.

"And I will escort you outside. If anyone asks, I was suffering from insomnia and stress because of current circumstances." Tyran bent down to press a tender kiss to the crown of Phaedra's mass of bright pink curls. "It pains me to be away from my mate and our unborn child."

Braxon pointedly cleared his throat.

"Oh, and my *anrik*, too." Tyran smiled and reached down to Braxon, drawing the other male to his feet. The two of them embraced and exchanged a brief but fiery kiss that seemed to raise the temperature of the room several degrees.

"Of course, my prince. We'll make sure the explanation reaches the right ears."

Tariq gathered up the few items of medical equipment they'd used to do the scans and put them away while Jody gave the threesome a few more instructions and plenty of encouragement. The last few weeks of a pregnancy seemed to be the most difficult, especially for first-time parents. From now until the child was born, she expected a steady increase in calls, questions, and reassurances.

It was one of her favorite aspects of the job, and judging by the smiles on Sulat and Tariq's faces, it was something they enjoyed, too.

It was a good way to end the evening. Not that her day was over. Jody already knew she'd spend the night going over everything, wondering what she could have done better, and preparing for what she'd do next.

7

Sleep didn't come easily for Sulat. He tossed and turned for hours, his mind caught in a loop as he reviewed the evening's events over and over again.

When he did fall asleep, his dreaming mind diverged from reality, creating a fantasy so perfect a part of him knew it was a dream even as he let it unfold.

That brief kiss he'd stolen from her had only been the first. Instead of going to check on their patient, he'd flown her back to his home. Then he'd taken her in his arms under the star-strewn sky.

Yes. More.

Their clothes melted away, and he reveled at having her naked in his arms. He claimed her mouth with hard kisses fueled by hunger while she draped her arms around his neck. Her bare breasts were pressed to his chest as he plumbed the depths of her mouth with his tongue. She straddled his thigh, writhing as she ground her sex against him.

"Sulat. Please. I want you." Her words inflamed him.

They kissed again, and somehow, they were in bed together. His bed.

Jody lay beneath him with her legs around his waist, one hand reaching behind him to stroke the spot between his wings that always...*Yes!*

He drove himself into her, his cock buried to the hilt in the velvet heat of her pussy. One thrust, two, he was almost there.

He awoke with aching balls and a rock-hard cock.

Qarf! Even in his dreams he couldn't have her.

Frustrated, he flung off the covers and walked to the bathing room next door. Maybe a hot shower and a jerk-off session would help clear his head enough to let him sleep. Maybe.

He managed a few hours, but with wakefulness came the sense that he'd missed out on something important. Jody.

It was obvious now that his attraction to the human female ran deeper than he'd realized. Much deeper. Why hadn't he noticed? Had he been deliberately ignoring the obvious? Possibly. More likely he'd been focused on Tariq's darkening mood and hadn't consciously registered the depth of his interest in the human doctor... or her apparent interest in him. Or was it them? He didn't have enough information to know.

He mulled things over during his morning shower and came to several conclusions. He was irked with himself for missing the painfully obvious and even more annoyed with Tariq.

The two of them had always been drawn to the same females, which meant Tariq was likely as interested in

Chapter 7

Jody as he was. So why was the stubborn *mogat* resisting? Was this the real reason behind his dour mood of late?

Sulat thought back to the moment they had left the palace together. They couldn't discuss anything about Phaedra's situation in case someone was listening. That left them talking in vague terms about stomach ailments and possible ways to alleviate stress and insomnia.

It hadn't felt right to be talking about such things out loud and in public, but it was necessary. Not only because they needed the invented reason for their nocturnal visit to spread but because Jody wasn't implanted with the tech that allowed he and Tariq to speak privately.

Thinking back, tension had crept in even before they reached the palace gate, the three of them lapsing into silence once they were out of potential earshot. No one spoke until they'd reached the street.

He'd offered to escort her home, but Jody had declined. He thought he saw a hint of regret in her eyes, he couldn't be sure. Human expressions were something he was still learning to understand.

"I'll see you soon," was what he'd said as she entered the autonomous vehicle she'd called to take her home.

Again, that flicker of *something* in her eyes, and then she was gone, the moment lost.

The memory made him wince. He hadn't been that awkward around a female in a century or so. The moment they'd found Raenia and the *sharhal*—the mating fever—had taken them, he'd lost all interest in other females. That was how it was for his species. Once they found their mate the bond was both intense and immediate, making courtship rituals unnecessary.

He scowled as it dawned on him that if he wanted Jody, he'd have to learn how humans managed to find mates. Since he had no intention of asking his daughter about it, he'd have to do some research on his own.

He was still deep in thought when he wandered into the kitchen in search of food and a hot cup of *kabari*.

On the counter next to the food replicator was a data tablet, its screen flashing yellow. Raenia used to leave reminders and messages that way, ensuring he and Tariq would get the prompt even if she'd got lost in her work and forgot all about whatever it was.

Smiling at the memory, Sulat picked up the tablet and tapped the screen to activate the message. His smile faded the moment he saw Tariq's face on the screen. His *anrik* looked haggard, which was not a common state when one had nanotech actively enhancing every cell in their body.

The look in his eyes worried Sulat the most. Frustration warred with a deep sadness he hadn't seen since the early days after Raenia's death.

"We need to talk. Meet me at the main practice arena. I'll be waiting."

Qarf.

Sulat scrubbed a hand over his face and groaned. It had been decades since they'd done this. He could almost hear Raenia scolding them, her beautiful face marred with worry and frustration. "You're grown males. Why do you insist on continuing this insane tradition of beating each other senseless whenever you disagree?"

She'd never understood that sometimes the easiest way to have a hard conversation involved nonlethal violence.

Sulat was halfway to his room when it struck him that thinking about Raenia didn't hurt the same way it used to. Oh, the grief was still there, but it was muted and distant now, like a storm that had passed overhead and moved on, leaving only faint rumbles of thunder in its destructive wake.

"And that is the *fraxxing* problem." For him, the storm had passed, but Tariq was still inside the maelstrom, and Sulat feared his *anrik* had decided to stay there.

He mulled that idea over as he changed outfits and mentally prepared for the fight to come. Maybe now they'd finally clear the air and find a way forward.

"I should have slugged him the first time we had this conversation... it would have saved us some time and a lot of *qarfing* frustration."

~

It only took a few minutes to fly to the arena. From the air he spotted several groups practicing aerial combat, diving and dodging through the open arches of the arena as they tried to gain an advantage over their opponents.

Some used daggers and other bladed weapons, their edges dulled to prevent serious injury. More and more participants used *kestarvs*. The old-fashioned weapon had returned to favor of late. The newly formed rangers used a variation of the expandable staff so it was also an energy weapon.

He still preferred his daggers, though today he'd be using blunted ones.

Tension settled into his muscles and mind, putting his senses on high alert and making his body ready for combat even before he passed through the energy field that encapsulated the entire building, keeping out the elements while still allowing beings to push through with only minimal resistance.

"*I'm here,*" he sent the message to Tariq.

"*I've signed us both in and reserved a sparring area. West corner. Ground floor.*"

He took a moment to find an empty locker in the changing room and placed anything he didn't need inside. Wearing only pants, boots, and a pair of daggers sheathed and strapped to his forearms, he made his way onto the heart of the arena.

Hard-packed golden sand covered the floor, providing firm footing and a *slightly* softer landing surface to anyone knocked from the air. At least, that's what he'd been told, but personal experience suggested the only ones who believed the sand cushioned anything had never fallen onto it.

He circled around the outside of the arena, careful to watch overhead for falling objects like dislodged armor, weapons, and occasional bodies. This might be called a practice arena, but it still held its dangers. That thought lingered in his mind as Sulat caught sight of his *anrik*.

Tariq stood, shoulders squared and arms crossed over his chest, in the space he'd reserved. They'd be tucked

Chapter 7

into a corner, beneath an overhang that provided shelter and privacy while limiting the users' ability to fly. It was exactly the kind of place they'd had some of their harshest *discussions* over their time together.

The gear he wore was as well-worn and battered as his own, though Tariq's looked like it hadn't been cleaned or oiled in some time. Still, it would serve its purpose—deflect and soften the impact of the blows about to be exchanged.

"Took you long enough," Tariq grumbled, his entire body tense with barely contained emotions.

"I slept late. You know I've never been one for early mornings." He waited a beat before adding, "But we're not here to banter. Are we, Riq?"

"We're not."

Sulat rolled his shoulders and settled his weight on the balls of his feet before speaking again. "Speak your truth, Tariq. It's long past time we had this talk."

"My truth?" Tariq almost spat out the question. "My truth is the same as yours. We lost the one female we were meant to love. We should live the rest of our lives alone."

"And that's the problem. You think we're in agreement on this, but we're not." Sulat narrowed the distance between them and opened his hands, palms outward. "We've never had this conversation."

"We did. We moved to Haven so we could mourn in peace and solitude. The agreement didn't change. You did! You're letting your cock guide your thinking. And no matter how intriguing or lovely Jody is, she's a wingless, soft-skinned human!"

Tariq moved before he finished speaking, rushing Sulat with fists raised.

The first exchange of blows was explosive, wild swings and undisciplined punches fueled by raw emotion on both sides.

"It's not just my cock that's interested in Jody." He timed the words to land between blows. "And don't think I didn't hear you say she *was lovely and intriguing.*" Exertion made the last few words come out as a snarl.

"Of course you'd focus on that bit and nothing else I said." Tariq hammered him with several hard jabs to the ribs, leaving him too breathless to retort. Instead, Sulat extended his wings, flapping them hard enough to lift him up and back, out of his *anrik's* reach.

Tariq hissed in frustration and lunged at him again, but this time Sulat sidestepped in time to avoid the charge and catch his breath. "I heard what you said. What I want to know is why you're so intent on riding the winds of our grief for the rest of your life? Raenia was the sun that lit our sky, but there are other lights in the universe."

The next attack came so fast he barely had time to raise him arms to block the barrage of blows. "Is that what you tell yourself? When she died, I lost all the light in my life." Tariq's pain drenched every word he uttered, leaving Sulat stunned. This wasn't what he'd expected to hear today. Though maybe it should have been.

Sulat went on the offensive, using words instead of his fists. "You didn't lose everything, you stubborn *bakaffa*. I'm still here, and so is our daughter. Vixi's light is as bright as her mother's. If you are lost in the dark, it's not because you're alone in the present. It's because you're choosing to dwell in the shadows of the past!"

Tariq lunged again, and this time Sulat caught a glint of metal as it flashed through the air. Their fight had escalated to blades already? So be it.

He drew his own weapons in time to parry his *anrik's* attack. There was no real threat. The blades were dulled and Tariq hadn't seen the inside of a practice arena in so long his reflexes and endurance lagged behind his.

"It's all I deserve," Tariq said.

"What *you* deserve?" Sulat snarled and swiped with his blade, striking Tariq's flank with bruising force. "Has grief made you blind? Or are you too stubborn to see beyond your pain? I don't understand why you are determined to punish yourself, but I do know this. You are dragging Vixi and me along with you."

They both lapsed into silence, too busy trying to score a hit to speak. Sulat focused on the small details— the hiss of sand beneath booted feet, the rhythm of Tariq's breathing, the thud of flesh striking flesh punctuated by the occasional ring of clashing blades.

He caught Tariq with a vicious backhanded blow that made the other male stagger to one side. In the brief respite Sulat regained enough breath to speak. "Why, Riq?"

Tariq spat out a mouthful of blood and glared. "Because it was my fault. She's gone because of me."

"By all the winds that blow, is *that* what's been eating at you?" Sulat charged again, slamming his shoulder into Tariq's stomach and driving him off his feet.

To counter, Tariq flared his wings for balance and

crashed both hands down on Sulat's back, hitting him in the vulnerable spot on his back. The blow sent a white spike of pain down his spine, immobilizing him long enough for Tariq to put some distance between them.

"I knew there were storms in the forecast. We shouldn't have gone flying."

"Like you had a choice," Sulat hissed as soon as he had enough air in his lungs to speak. "Or have you forgotten that Raenia was as stubborn as you and as spirited as our little whirlwind? You weren't her keeper, Riq. She made her own decisions."

"And one of them got her killed. That's on me."

Sulat straightened but didn't move to restart their fight. "I was there too. I told you both to go and enjoy some time together. Do you think I don't regret that? I wanted you both out of the house so I could have some peace and quiet. I never thought..." Sulat's throat tightened. "I never imagined. I needed a few hours of solitude. Not a lifetime."

For the first time since they'd started this damned fight the two of them locked gazes.

Tariq uttered a low, pained chuckle. "You blame yourself?"

"I did, but eventually I accepted that this wasn't anyone's fault. A terrible thing happened. We lost her. I grieved. I railed against the winds of fate, but eventually?" Sulat sighed and lowered his blades. "Eventually I realized that Raenia wouldn't want us to mourn forever. Winds and tides, can you imagine what she'd say to us if she could see us right now?"

Tariq snorted with derisive laughter and then

groaned and wrapped one arm around one side of his chest. "She'd call us names, stamp her foot the way she did when she was utterly furious, and threaten to string us up by our wings."

"Didn't she do that to you once?"

Tariq actually grinned. "*That* was entirely consensual."

He walked over and placed a gentle hand on his *anrik's* shoulder. "I miss her too. Every day."

Tariq turned to look at him, his expression sharp. "Then why are you trying to replace her?" Even has he said it, something in his hard expression changed, as if hearing the words spoken aloud granted him some missing insight.

Sulat stayed quiet and let the moment play out.

"*Qarf*. I really am an idiot. Of course you don't want to replace our Raenia."

"For a brilliant healer, you can be remarkably dense at times."

This time the glare shot his way was full of wry humor. "Asshole."

"Does this mean I can put the blades away? Or do I need to beat you up a little more?" Sulat asked.

"That's what you think happened here? You're wrong, my friend. I was clearly beating you." Tariq swiped at his split lip with the back of his free hand and scowled at the fresh blood that stained his scales.

"I'm not the one bleeding," Sulat pointed out.

"Oh, you are," Tariq said smugly.

Startled, Sulat checked himself over and cursed when he discovered blood trickling down his side from a set of slash marks that started on his back and trailed over his side. "How?" he started to ask but then answered his own question. "You got me with your claws, you sneaky bastard."

Now he knew about the injury he couldn't ignore the discomfort anymore. Sharp pain from the slashes rose in his awareness accompanied by a litany of smaller aches and bruises.

"You know," he groaned as he took inventory of his injuries. "I'm starting to think Raenia was right. There has to be an easier way to make you talk about your feelings."

"My feelings? This was about both of us. You never told me you felt guilty for encouraging us to go out that day."

"And you failed to mention how you felt, too." He glanced skyward. "Sorry, *mahaya*, we are still too stubborn to do this any other way." Sulat looked over at Tariq. "We still need to address one more topic."

Tariq nodded. "Jody."

"Jody," Sulat repeated. "I want to follow that wind and see where it carries me. The question is, will you be with me, or do I make this flight alone?"

He braced for the worst, but Tariq surprised him. "Give me a few days to think about it. We have always been attracted to the same females, and that hasn't changed." His *anrik* rubbed the back of his neck. "Do you have any idea how to even make a romantic overture to a human female?"

"Some. It involves meals, conversation, and plants."

"Plants? Why plants?" Tariq asked.

"I'm not sure. Vixi mentioned something about it."

"We'll find someone else to ask. Our daughter has already made her thoughts known. If we do this." Tariq raised a hand. "And I do mean *if*. We work through it without any help from Vixi."

"Agreed." Sulat made a show of dusting himself off. "She'd shed her scales if she could see us right now."

"It's not *my* scales you should be worried about."

Qarf. "Vixi? What are you doing here?" both of them asked at almost the same time.

Their daughter stepped out of a shadowy corner, her scowl a perfect replica of Tariq's. "Funny thing. Several of my friends contacted me to let me know my fathers were beating each other senseless in public."

Sulat looked around for the first time since the fight began. They'd attracted an audience. The usual sounds of the arena were silenced, and all attention was on them and their small corner.

"We were practicing. That's what this space is for," Tariq tried to explain.

Vixi flared her wings in annoyance. "Practicing. Right. I'm not a child anymore. Don't treat me like one. I know what you were doing, and I can make a fair bet on the reason why."

From somewhere in the back, someone called out. "Damn, you're cute when you get riled, Vixi. After you finish dealing with your fathers, you should have a drink with us."

Sulat whipped out a dagger and pointed it in the general direction of the voice. "Find somewhere else to be. Now. All of you. Especially whoever made that last comment."

The same voice whooped with laughter. This time, he recognized it. So did Tariq. "Cam Allen, I know that was you. Stay away from our daughter."

Vixi waved the others off. "You don't have any say in my love life, Fathers. Not when you're making a spectacle of yourselves trying to figure out your own. Go home, get cleaned up and do something about the blood and bruises. We'll talk later." She turned and walked away.

"Where are you going?" Sulat asked.

"To get a drink with Cam and his friends," she replied without turning around or even slowing down.

He and Tariq sighed and made their way to the exit, both of them doing their best to walk tall despite their battered bodies. The temporary pain was worth it, though. The two of them were finally on the same flight path. It was about *fraxxing* time.

8

Five days. She'd been avoiding Tariq and Sulat for the better part of a week. Jody knew she needed to deal with it, but she'd rather be dropped into a pen of starving *gharshtu* than face Tariq and Sulat right now.

This wasn't the way she wanted things to go, but after she heard about their brawl at the local arena, what other choice did she have? Everyone in the colony seemed to have an opinion on the matter. Most thought it amusing and seemed to enjoy relaying every detail, real or invented. Some expressed curiosity about what the fight was about and offered up their personal theories.

Jody had a damned good idea what the fight was about. *Her.* Which was why she'd kept her distance from both males and their daughter despite the fact she worked with them all in some capacity. She'd handled her administrative work from home, rearranged her hours at the clinic, and taken efforts to arrive at the new arrivals integration camp during periods she knew Vixi was busy elsewhere.

So far, it had worked, though Lores made sly remarks about it every chance she could. Beneath her teasing and sometimes caustic remarks was an undertone of concern Jody appreciated.

"I'll figure it out today," she muttered as she made her way to the clinic. Dodging the last remnants of puddles left by last night's rain. The early morning weather was clear and bright, though, lifting her spirits despite the lingering chill in the air.

Haven's streets and sidewalks were quiet at this time of the day, but a handful of beings were already out and about. Some prepared their stores and businesses for opening while others were on their way to work on coming home from a night shift. She smiled at those she recognized but never slowed her pace. Not until she spotted the small crowd gathered around the front door of the clinic.

So many patients this early? Had there been an accident? Another outbreak of illness? And why were they all outside?

She hurried forward, her mind filled with questions she couldn't answer yet.

Once she was close enough, she called out to the group of Vardarians gathered outside her clinic. "I'm here. What's the issue? Who needs help first?"

Some turned toward her, wearing similar expressions of worry or even fear. Others shied away, leaving the area with their heads down and wings partially extended, as if they might take flight any second.

She didn't shift her focus to the damage until she was certain none of them needed aid.

Chapter 8

What the hell?

The windows and doors of her clinic had been vandalized—not with paint or even a laser etching device but with something more disturbing. The air reeked of chemicals that stung her nose and made her eyes water. Despite her blurred vision, Jody saw that a single symbol appeared repeatedly, identical in size and still smoking slightly from whatever acid had been used.

Something about the glyph, which looked to her like a series of swirling lines inside a circular border, tickled the back of her brain. She'd seen it before but where? She shoved that question aside. It could wait until she'd dealt with more urgent issues. Like getting inside to check for damage to the clinic itself.

Part of her wanted to call Sulat and ask him to accompany her. However, if she did that, not only would she have to wait, but once he arrived there'd be all sorts of awkwardness since she'd been ignoring his attempts to contact her.

No, the best thing to do was to deal with this herself, at least for now. With her decision made, Jody tapped the keypad next to the door, careful to stay as far as possible from the damaged areas and whatever chemical residue might linger on the surface.

Her code activated the usual chime, and the pad flashed to indicate access granted, but the door didn't move.

She tried again. This time something in the wall made a grinding noise that set her teeth on edge, but nothing else happened.

Dammit. She needed to get in there.

Out of options, Jody pressed the button marked "Emergency."

"Please state your name and nature of the emergency," Rae's voice came through a small speaker Jody hadn't noticed.

"Rae, it's Dr. Clark. I need you to open the door."

A few seconds passed. "I'm sorry, Dr. Clark. The door appears to be malfunctioning. Would you like me to open the emergency exit?"

"Yes, please." The other door was designed to be opened from inside, which was why she hadn't tried it first.

Only a handful of beings still loitered in the area. They clustered together, all watching her with wary curiosity as she jogged around to the side.

The door opened before she reached it, and she rushed straight in. "Rae, is the clinic empty?" she asked, only after she was inside. "Damn, I probably should have asked you that before I barreled in here."

That little voice in the back of her head repeated its desire to have Sulat and even Tariq present right now. She ignored it. It was too late for that, and she was more than capable of dealing with this on her own. This was how she'd managed for years now, alone.

"You are the only occupant, Dr. Clark," Rae said, the AI's voice pulling her out of her thoughts.

"Okay, good. Did they get inside? Is anything damaged?"

Rae's hologram formed a few meters away and fixed Jody with a look of concern. "I don't understand the question. Who were you expecting? Why would anyone damage the clinic?"

Jody exhaled softly with relief. "I'm happy to hear that. It means everything inside is as it should be."

Rae cocked her head to one side. "Which implies things outside are not as they should be. What happened?"

"Vandals. They etched the windows and main door with some kind of acid. That's why the door wouldn't open. I guess the mechanism was damaged by whatever they used to create the symbols." She frowned. "Wait. Are you telling me you don't have any idea what happens beyond the walls of the clinic?"

"I do not. Each of my manifestations is limited to the clinic or med-bay they are assigned to."

"I understand that, but why don't you have any way of knowing what happens to the clinic you're assigned to?"

"My job is to oversee the clinic and aid the healers in their duties. Security was not part of my original program."

"Remind me to bring that up with someone in security. That seems like a serious oversight."

"I have checked my files. This is the first time anything like this has happened since I came online. I doubt my creator considered it a possibility." Rae paused before adding. "I'm not sure who you could discuss this matter with. The colony does not have a designated security force."

"Right. I should have remembered that. Vardarian society is very different from human in some ways. More civilized, I guess. Vandalizing buildings of any kind is common in human settlements."

She had few choices available. The rangers were more concerned with areas outside the city, and calling on the palace guards would likely mean dealing with the unpleasant guard captain from the other night. She'd rather not do that, which meant contacting Spymaster Yardan. Given her connection to Phaedra, he'd want to know about this incident, anyway. Not that she thought the two things were related.

"Rae, I know this isn't part of your usual functions, but could you contact Yardan and invite him to view the damage? Oh, and you should probably tell Healers A'Nir and Vana, too. They'll want to know."

"I am messaging the spymaster now. Healer A'Nir has already been informed and will be here shortly." Rae's expression softened. "I know you've been avoiding him, but he is the senior healer for this colony."

"I'm not *avoiding* anyone," she said defensively. It was a bald-faced lie, and she regretted it immediately, even if the one she lied to was just a complex bit of coding with a face.

"It's possible I was trying to give him space after an incident that occurred a few days ago, but how did you know that?"

"All scheduling changes go through me. Your alterations all showed a similar pattern—a desire to avoid contact with two particular healers."

She could have sworn the AI actually smirked for a millisecond or two. "And he's on his way here? *Now?*"

"Yes. As I mentioned, I have no way of observing

anything outside these walls, so I cannot inform you of their exact arrival. Not until they enter... Oh. They're here," Rae announced before her hologram faded from sight.

"Thanks for the information," Jody drawled and then turned back the way she'd come while leaning into a lifetime of experience to smooth her features into a calm, confident mask. If the doctor looked calm, the patients tended to relax. No one wanted to be treated by someone who didn't at least look like they knew what they were doing.

"Jody!" Tariq called out as he hurried toward her. "You shouldn't have entered the clinic on your own."

"It's my clinic. Rae confirmed no one was inside." She didn't mention that she hadn't asked for that information before rushing in.

Tariq stopped a few steps away from her, his expression one of frantic concern. For *her*? The realization made her heart beat faster as heat rose in her cheeks.

Because things weren't awkward enough already.

That was the moment the *something* niggling at the back of her head screamed and waved its nonexistent arms, demanding her attention. The symbol meant something—something dangerous. That's why Tariq was so concerned.

Sulat rushed in, looking as worried as Tariq. *Veth.* Maybe she should have listened to the little voice earlier.

"Are you alright, *zurya*? Why are no guards with you?"

"What guards? As Rae reminded me, Haven doesn't

have anything like that. Who should I have called to report what I thought was just an act of vandalism?"

Both males gaped at her, opened mouthed and speechless for several seconds. It should have made them look foolish, but somehow they still looked unthinkably handsome. How was that possible? It had to be all in her head, and that meant her head wasn't where it needed to be.

"Vandalism?" Tariq shook his head. "If only that was the case."

"That symbol." Jody twirled one hand in the air as she drew a series of diminishing spirals. "What does it mean?"

"It's a warning. A serious one. The *Liq'za* have targeted you."

Of course. The *Liq'za* were all about the purity of the Vardarian race and culture. They had threatened Phaedra and her baby, forcing the princess into hiding. Now, the same zealots were after her.

For a moment a chill of fear wrapped icy fingers around her soul and squeezed. Her breath caught, her hands clenched, and every muscle in her body screamed at her to get away from here.

The hell with that.

Anger burned white hot, melting the chill of fear in seconds. "So, they think I'll turn tail and run because they etched a few glyphs on my clinic? Is this their first time going after humans? It must be because that's not going to work."

Tariq actually smiled at her and then at Sulat. "Your *zurya* has petals of steel."

Wait. What? Had Tariq just called her Sulat's blossom, complimented her, and managed to *smile*, too?

"She is not mine," Sulat said, "since neither of us has had a chance to speak to her on the subject. This is not the time or place for it, either."

"Definitely not," Jody agreed. "Let's focus on getting the clinic up and running. Later, we can talk."

Later, when she'd had a chance to sort out her feelings—about the vandalism, the implied threat, and Tariq's unexpected change of heart. She'd expected them to still be working through the issues she'd caused. For *fraxx* sake, by all reports, they'd beaten each other senseless only a few days ago.

Only one thing could help her make sense of everything at a time like this—a glass of chocolate milk and a batch of homemade cookies. Pity neither was available right now.

"But later, cookies," she muttered to herself.

"What was that?" Sulat asked.

"Cookies are my coping mechanism, and right now, I could use a dozen or so. Too bad I don't have any."

"Ha! Tariq has a stash of them in his office. In fact, I believe they're programmed into the food replicator under his name."

Tariq tipped his head and looked down at her as if judging her worth, though she saw a surprising twinkle in his green eyes. "Are you a devotee, or simply a dabbler like this one?" He jerked his thumb toward Sulat. "Because dabblers do not get the best of my stash."

"Sulat, is this true?" She shot him a look of dramatic disappointment, enjoying the moment of lighthearted banter despite the circumstances. "How could you not appreciate the delicious artistry of a properly made cookie?"

He laughed as he answered. "I am clearly an imperfect male. One who hopes you will overlook his flaws."

"I'll consider it after we discuss your feelings about chocolate. But that's a conversation for another time."

Tariq gestured for her to follow him. "I think this day requires both cookies and coffee. Come with me."

"We're going to sit and have coffee? What about the clinic? The threat?"

Sulat tapped a spot behind his ear. "We've heard from Spymaster Yardan. He's on his way and has a contingent of palace guards with him. For now, he'd like us to stay put. He has questions for you, and I imagine he intends to assign you a protection detail."

"How can I do my job with guards standing around all day? They'll intimidate my patients and get in my way."

Both males smiled sympathetically.

"Spoken like a true healer," Tariq said.

"If it makes you feel any better, he'll probably do the same to us," Sulat added.

"Oh no. Have you been threatened, too?" she asked.

"Not yet, but I assume it's only a matter of time." Tariq lifted one wing in a shrug. "They won't stop until they accomplish their goals, or they're caught and executed for their actions."

"Normally I am opposed to capital punishment, but I'd make an exception in this case. Threatening a mother's and child's lives because of their genetics is obscene."

"You'll hear no argument from us." Sulat moved past them. "But no more discussion until after I have a hot cup of *kabari* in my hands. This morning started much too early for my liking."

"Excuse him," Tariq said with fond amusement. "My *anrik* doesn't function well until closer to midday."

"Because mornings are horrible things that should be outlawed across the known worlds," Sulat called back just before moving out of sight.

Jody turned to Tariq, determined to say the right thing even if this wasn't the right time. "I'm sorry."

"Why? This wasn't your fault. This is the *Liq'za's* doing."

"Oh, no. I'm not talking about this morning. I meant I'm sorry I caused problems between the two of you. I... I heard about the fight."

"Ah." Tariq's expression turned rueful as he moved closer. "Whatever you heard, it was no doubt exaggerated. Sulat and I have always worked out our differences that way."

The questions popped out before she could stop herself. "You have? Why, in the name of gravity, would you do that?"

"If she were here, Raenia would tell you it's because we're stubborn, foolish males."

"If your *mahaya* were here, the two of you wouldn't be fighting. That's the problem. Isn't it? My behavior instigated Sulat's kiss, and you didn't approve. I respect your decision, Tariq. I'll do my best to make sure that doesn't happen again."

Tariq growled low in his throat.

She stepped backward, but he caught her wrist and gripped it.

"No. You are not to blame. In fact, I owe you an apology for *my* actions. I was, and still am, coming to terms with some aspects of Raenia's death."

He bowed his head, and for a moment she saw behind the mask he wore. Traces of sadness drew down the corners of his mouth, but the haunted look in his eyes caught her attention.

She knew that look. It was the one she saw in the mirror every time she lost a patient. The doubt, regret, and constant questioning. Had she done all she could? What could she have done better?

She covered his hand with her free one and squeezed, offering silent support. In the moment that followed, her own regret and worries about the damage she thought she'd done to the two males' friendship fell away.

~

He'd been such a *bakaffa*. Tariq saw that now. He'd done the very thing he counseled his patients not to do—allow themselves to be drawn into a web of dark whispers and doubts. The healer had failed to heal himself, and in doing so, he'd hurt so many, including Jody. She didn't deserve his anger or resentment. She was kind, capable, and… he'd finally admitted to himself, extremely attractive. Guilt over his interest in her had consumed his thoughts and sent him soaring into the depths of a dangerous storm.

"You are blameless in this. I was wrong, and I am truly sorry for the way I've acted." He glanced down at her hand where it covered his. Her touch was gentle, and he briefly wondered what it would feel like to have her touch him in other places. That simple thought caused the wall he'd built around his desires to crack and crumble. Years of need crashed over him, and for a moment, he lost control.

One moment they were two beings sharing a moment of compassion. The next, his arm was around her waist as he pulled her up against his body.

If she'd resisted, he might have found the strength to stop, but she came to him willingly, with her head up, eyes wide, and lips parted in surprise.

He released her wrist and moved to cup her soft cheek in his hand.

"Tariq?" she spoke his name as a question.

"If you're asking what I'm doing, I don't have an answer." He smiled and stroked his thumb across her lips. "It might be I'm losing my mind."

She smiled, her cheeks warming beneath his fingers as she nestled against his chest.

"Lost your mind? No. You've finally found it again. Qarf, it took you long enough," Sulat spoke through their internal link.

"Drink your *kabari*," Tariq shot back, speaking aloud.

"Tell Sulat if he has something to say, he should come out here and join us," Jody said with a light riff of laughter.

Sulat reappeared, grinning and almost radiating smugness. "Did my *zurya* call for me?"

"She did." Jody reached a hand toward Sulat. "I'm not sure how this works, but I do know one thing. Whatever happens, we are in it together. All three of us."

Sulat moved behind Jody, pressing her between them. It wasn't the same as holding Raenia, and nothing ever would be. Being with Jody would be an adventure of a different kind.

Why had it taken him so long to understand that?

Sulat growled in frustration. "Stop thinking, Riq. Now's not the time. If you don't *fraxxing* kiss her this second, I will."

It was good advice, so he took it, bending down to taste the lush promise of Jody's lips. Soft. Sweet. Warm. Kissing her was like flying on a spring breeze.

Her mouth parted beneath his as she rose on her toes, one hand clutching at the fabric of his top as she kissed him back. Heat and need bloomed deep in his chest. His blood sang and his cock went harder than hull plating in an instant.

He slanted his lips over hers, exploring the curve of her mouth until need drove him to take the kiss deeper. Jody moaned, the sound vibrating against his lips and tongue.

Why had he denied himself this pleasure for so long? He couldn't recall right now.

"Don't get greedy," Sulat muttered. "She's mine too."

Jody laughed again. "We'll discuss who belongs to whom another time. Kiss now. Talk later."

She nipped at his lower lip a second later. "Which means you need to let go of me for now."

"For now," he growled. One taste of her wasn't nearly enough, but Sulat deserved this, too. Probably more than he did.

Tariq loosened his hold enough to allow Jody to turn around, her soft body rubbing against his with every motion. Once she faced Sulat, Tariq moved in closer, his cock pressed against the curve of her back.

She fit between them perfectly, melding the three of them together so tightly he felt her moan as Sulat claimed her mouth.

Still hungry for more, Tariq kept one hand on her hip as he reached up with the other to release her hair from its confining bun. Curls tumbled down around his fingers, and he dropped the hair clip in his hurry to tangle his fingers in the silken cascade.

"Spymaster Yardan has arrived and requested access via the back door. Shall I let him in?" Rae asked.

Sulat cursed almost as loudly as Tariq at the AI's intrusion. She made a distressed noise and wriggled out from between them. She flashed them a fleeting, rueful smile and hurried toward the breakroom, her hands already busy smoothing out her rumpled clothes and hair.

"To be continued!" Sulat called after her. Once she was out of sight, he glared at Tariq. "So much time wasted because you wouldn't talk about your feelings. I should have punched you weeks ago."

He flicked two fingers up in an obscene gesture toward his anrik but directed his response to the AI. "Rae, please open the door for Spymaster Yardan."

"Of course. If you take him to the break room, I believe Dr. Clark is preparing a snack and beverages."

"Cookies, no doubt," Sulat said. "I'll give her a hand."

"You do that." He turned and walked down the corridor. "Rae, please access my personal replicator files and have it create a batch of my favorites to go with the ones Dr. Clark is making."

There was a brief pause before Rae answered, which was unusual. "I took the liberty of copying that recipe over to her files a few minutes ago. I thought you would want her to have access to such things."

He almost tripped over his own feet. "You thought..." He set out again, only a few meters from the door now. "Is that your way of saying you approve of Dr. Clark—of Jody?"

"I am a machine intelligence with no opinion on such matters. Emotions are not part of my programming."

He had his own thoughts on that. Raenia had imbued the AI with more of her personality than anyone thought was possible... or permissible. If the AI approved? It was as close as he could ever come to having their *mahaya's* blessing.

Before he could process anything further, the door opened and the prince's personal spymaster stepped through. The male filled the hall with his presence in a way few others could.

"This day has barely started and I'm already unhappy with the way it's progressing. This wasn't the *Liq'za's* only target. The Bar None, Earthly Delights, and several other businesses owned or operated by humans were targeted."

"Businesses but not their homes?"

Yardan scowled. "No homes. Not yet. But I'm expecting things to escalate over the next while. I have theories, but this is not the place to discuss them."

The big male glanced down the hall. "How is Dr. Clark handling this?"

"Furious and ready to fight," Tariq said.

"Good. So far, all the humans have reacted that way." Yardan's face cracked into a rare smile. "These *Liq'za* have no idea who they're messing with. The humans continue to surprise me. They are almost as fierce as Vardarians."

"So I am discovering."

Yardan actually grinned. "I noticed. Or did you think I missed your rumpled clothes and the fact her scent is all over you?"

"That is none of your business, Spymaster. Go use your powers of observation on someone else." Tariq waved him down the corridor. "She's in the breakroom with Sulat."

With a nod, Yardan headed in the indicated direction. As he passed by, he murmured softly. "Keep her close, Healer, and be careful who you trust."

As the spymaster's warning sank in, a fire kindled deep in Tariq's chest. He hadn't felt it since the day Raenia died. He would protect Jody from the coming storm for one simple reason. She may not be his *mahaya*, but she was something equally important.

She was *his*. How that could be didn't matter. He knew in his heart it was the truth.

9

How could a day be simultaneously one of her worst *and* one of her best? It boggled her mind, but that didn't change the facts. Yes, she was the target of a xenophobic secret society, but she'd also found herself in both Sulat and Tariq's arms and shared kisses that had set her soul on fire.

Even the hours-long interview with the prince's spymaster hadn't been much of a strain. The male had asked questions about her every move and experience for the last few weeks, asking her to recall details that had already faded. She wasn't sure why he needed half of the information he'd asked for, but she trusted there was a reason.

Tariq and Sulat had stayed by her side the entire time, only stepping away to refill drinks or speak to Rae about rebooking patients or transferring them to another healer's roster.

She'd sent a quick message to Lores, telling her friend to stay home today and not to go out alone. A longer explanation would have to wait, though Jody was certain that by the time she got in touch again, Lores would know what happened. Haven might be unique in some ways, but gossip was still the fastest form of communication in the colony.

To her surprise, both Sulat and Tariq stayed with her after Yardan departed. Once it was clear they weren't leaving, she asked the obvious question. "Don't you both have things to do today? Patients to see, research to do, errands to run?"

"Not today," Sulat said.

"If you're worried about me, I'm touched. Really." She placed a hand over her heart in a gesture of gratitude. "I've been on my own a long time, and I'm used to having to take care of myself. I'll be fine."

"Yes, you will because we're not leaving your side until you are safe at home," Tariq said.

"With the guards Yardan promised to send standing watch outside," Sulat added.

Their concern for her was an unexpected pleasure, a warm and welcome feeling she wanted to bask in. If they intended to walk her home, this time she might get a goodbye kiss from each of them before they went on with their day.

She hadn't been able to get those first passionate kisses out of her mind all morning. Every time she looked at either of them, her libido lit up like an overheated jump-engine. It had to be the stress of the day making her feel this way. A few kisses shouldn't make her feel this way, even if they had been toe-curlingly good ones. She couldn't remember the last time she'd felt this way... but it had been a few decades, at least.

Forcing her mind back to the task at hand, she smiled at her companions. "I think I'm done here. Rae can transfer any files I need to my home office. I'll fetch my med-kit from the office and we can be on our way. Rae, please inform anyone who inquires to contact one of the other med-centers for assistance."

"Of course, Dr. Clark. If you need anything, please let me know."

"Thank you, I will. Oh, and Rae? I haven't forgotten. I'll speak to these two about providing some improvements to your security functions."

"That would be appreciated. Helping the healers and their patients is my primary purpose. Now I have registered this vulnerability, the inability to safeguard those under my care is... disconcerting."

"I imagine it would be."

A crew was already working on the front door as they passed through it. Everyone in sight wore crests and garb that marked them as members of the palace staff, all under the watchful eye of several royal guardsmen.

It wasn't until they left the area that she started to feel uneasy. The reality of her situation finally sank in as they moved through the now bustling streets. The crowd made her feel vulnerable. Were some of these beings part of the *Liq'za*? Did their friendly smiles hide dark secrets and intentions?

As if reading her mind, Sulat and Tariq each took one of her hands and moved in close to her sides. A second later they extended their wings, overlapping them to create a protective wall behind her.

She exhaled and gripped their hands tightly. "Thank you. I hate feeling this way. Suddenly I can't tell friend from foe."

"Most are friends who despise what the Liq'za stand for. The few who aren't..." Sulat's words trailed off into a threatening growl.

"If any of them try to harm you, we'll pay them back in kind," Tariq finished the statement.

"Healers and warriors." Jody shook her head. "I never imagined someone could be both. Not until I met the two of you."

Sulat shifted his grip on her hand so his thumb could stroke over the backs of her knuckles. "We fight to protect those we treasure. It is the way of our species."

Those we treasure. The words sent a thrill down her spine. It was too soon for those words to really be true, but they sparked hope for the future—a future that included all three of them.

"I'm on that list?" she asked, her tone light and teasing. "I'm honored, even though I'm certain Tariq's special cookies and of course, your daughter, are higher priorities."

"The recipe for those is a family tradition, passed down through centuries. They're definitely on the list," Tariq declared. "I'm glad you like them."

"I do. Very much. In fact, I think it's safe to say I've liked everything I've discovered about the two of you today."

"We feel the same way." Sulat raised her hand to his

mouth to kiss her fingers. "And for the record, I think you taste better than the cookies."

With that, the three of them departed. Despite the fact they walked instead of flew, Jody felt like her feet never touched the ground.

~

Her emotional high came crashing down the second she saw the symbols etched into the walls and door of her home. Not satisfied with defacing the clinic, the Liq'za had come to her house, too.

Feelings of violation mixed with utter fury. "Those bastards. They trashed my home!"

Both Tariq and Sulat growled in unison, their grip on her hands tightening.

"Stay with Tariq," Sulat told her firmly. "I'll check inside."

Part of her wanted to insist she come too, but what point was there? Seeing the damage wouldn't change anything, and if someone was still in there...

"Alright." She shifted closer to Tariq and released Sulat's hand. "But promise me you'll stay in contact with him while you're in there? He can relay what you say so I know what's going on."

"Agreed."

Sulat pulled a long-bladed knife from his belt as he stalked toward the front door, his footsteps almost completely silent. The smiling male she knew, the healer with a gentle bedside manner, had been replaced by a dangerous predator.

Tariq guided her to an open area where he could see anyone who approached. He kept one arm wrapped protectively around her shoulders, and his free hand rested on the pommel of his dagger. She'd always assumed the weapons were ceremonial. Apparently they served a more practical function, too.

"He's inside," Tariq said, his voice soft. "No one else appears to be there. He's going room to room to be sure."

"Did they damage anything?" Not that she had many possessions. The house had come with basic, practical furnishings. She'd only had time to add a few personal touches to the place.

"I'm sorry, *zurya*. They appear to have used more of that acidic compound to destroy the interior. Sulat doesn't think much can be salvaged."

She swallowed hard, not sure if the lump in her throat was due to anger or grief. "If it's safe for him, could he please look under my bed? I have a metal box stored there. Inside it are the only things that really matter to me." A stash of hard currency chips for emergencies. A few family keepsakes. A lock of Jacob's hair from his first haircut.

"Of course." Tariq relayed her request. She leaned into the solid support of Tariq's side as she waited for more news. He held her close, even extending one of his wings to shield her back. It helped.

A few minutes later he exhaled softly and squeezed her shoulders. "He has it and there's no serious damage. Your things are safe."

She sagged in relief. That box had traveled with her

for decades, full of keepsakes and memories she treasured. "Thank you. And thank Sulat."

"He's on his way out, now."

Tariq leaned over and kissed the top of her head. "I'm sure you've seen enough of Yarden today, but I've sent him a message. He needs to know what has happened."

"Of course he does. I just hope he doesn't ask all those questions again. It's not like my answers have changed since the last time we talked."

It had been a long day already, and it wasn't even noon yet. First the clinic, now this. How many other places had they hit? Yardan would know. This time, she had a few questions for him, too.

They only stayed long enough for Yardan to inspect the damage. Jody accompanied him, getting her first look at what remained of her home. They had dumped her furnishings into piles and doused them in acid, destroying everything. Glyphs appeared on all the walls, some etched, others obviously hand-painted in azure blue, the Vardarian color of mourning.

"They certainly weren't trying to be subtle," Yardan commented at one point as he shifted his wings to keep them far away from another pile of ruined furnishings.

His *mahaya*, Skye, cleared her throat pointedly, and the spymaster winced before looking at her. "I'm sorry, Dr. Clark. That was thoughtless of me. This is your home."

"I understand. While this is personal for me, you need to stay detached so you can see the bigger picture."

The cyborg female rolled her eyes. "That's what he

claims. I still think he can do his job and be nice at the same time."

Yardan looked over at Sulat and Tariq. "Females," he said with a hint of a grin. "I will never understand them."

Jody managed to gather up several undamaged items of clothing from a closet the vandals must have missed. She stuffed them into a bag, happy to at least have a change of clothing left to her name. Everything else could be replaced. That only left one question. Where was she sleeping tonight?

"For security reasons, do you think I should move into the palace?" she asked the group.

Tariq fixed her with a stern look, and Sulat actually growled. "You will not stay at the palace," Sulat said.

"You are coming home with us," Tariq stated.

The offer came as a shock. "Uh. I am?"

Skye's gaze moved from Tariq, to Sulat, to her, a smile growing on her face. "I know that tone. Probably best not to argue with them on this one, Dr. Clark. You won't win."

"And the palace isn't as safe as it should be," Yardan said.

Everyone turned to look at him, expecting more information.

"It's a theory, but I have my suspicions. I'd rather you weren't inside the palace walls right now." He gestured around them. "This could be a ploy to create enough concern that we moved you to the safest place on the planet."

She caught on immediately. "They're hoping I run straight to Phaedra's hiding place. It makes sense. Not only would I be safe there, but with the princess's due date coming up, it's logical I join her soon."

"Exactly."

Jody straightened her spine and nodded once. "If that's what they want, then *fraxx* them. I'm not giving them what they want."

"Damn right," Skye said approvingly.

"It's decided. You'll stay with us." Sulat made it sound like a royal decree.

"We will protect you," Tariq confirmed.

"And who is going to protect the two of you when the *Liq'za* adds you to their shit list?" Jody asked.

Skye answered before anyone else. "The rangers. I sent a message to Striker. You've met him. Right? Big cyborg. Doesn't speak much. Mated to Maggie from the Bar None. He leads the rangers, and he's already agreed to send over some cyborgs to act as security."

Yardan nodded. "It's a good idea. Right now it's safer to leave that job to someone the *Liq'za* would never recruit."

That worked for her, but she wasn't the only victim of the vile group. "What about Lores and the others? They'll need protection, too."

"I'm working on that. Lores, Vixi, and some of the others can move to the integration camp with the human women. There are more than enough habi-pods for that, and if most of them are in one place, which will simplify security." Skye's eyes hardened. "These assholes don't know who they're messing with. If they come for anyone in the colony, we'll make them regret it."

Tariq looked relieved. "Vixi will be protected? That's

good. She'd argue if we tried to make her stay with us. This way we can avoid that unpleasant scenario."

"Good." Yardan pointed toward the front door. "With that decided, I'd suggest the three of you go home and prepare to stay there for a while. There's a lot of work to do, and the sooner we have everyone safe and accounted for, the better."

"Agreed." Sulat took the bag of clothes from her and pulled the strap over his shoulder while tucking her box of treasures under his other arm.

"I'll carry your things. Riq will carry you."

Tariq confirmed the situation by opening his arms and then pointing to a spot in front of him. "Come here."

"But you... you don't like to fly. Are you sure?"

He cocked a brow in her direction. "Are you questioning me?"

Something in his tone made her pulse race. "No, Healer A'Nir. I would never do that."

As he drew her into his arms and reminded her to hang on, all she could hear was the roar of blood in her ears and Skye's laughter. "Good luck, Doc."

Jody clung to Tariq as he took off into the late morning sun. She had no idea what would happen next, but she was sure of one thing. She didn't need luck. Not when she had the two males she'd dreamed of since the first time they'd met.

10

Of all the scenarios he'd envisioned over the last few days, this one hadn't even been a consideration. Sulat couldn't decide if he wanted to scream at the ancestors for putting everyone he cared about at risk, or celebrate the fact Jody was coming home with them. It was a messy, twisted way to bring the three of them together, but it worked.

He spent the short flight home considering options and speaking to Tariq via their internal link. Not only did they put together a decent plan in that time, but it let him keep tabs on his *anrik*. Tariq had come a long way since their confrontation, but his healing was still in progress. Flying wouldn't be easy for him, but today he'd shown no signs of difficulty.

Once they were safely inside, Tariq did a full tour of the house to check that all the doors and windows were locked. While he did that, Sulat set down Jody's belongings and ushered her to a seat in the main living area.

She sat down with a grateful sigh and immediately started fixing her hair, trying to tame the wind-tangled curls. "Damn. I just realized I don't even own a comb anymore."

"Anything you need, we'll provide," Sulat said, moving in behind the chair she sat in. "May I help?"

She turned to look at him quizzically. From this angle, with her seated in a chair made for a much larger being, she looked even smaller than usual. "Help? You've already done that."

"And I will continue to do so. We both will. But I was referring to your hair."

"Oh." Her surprised expression was adorable. "You want to fix my hair for me?"

"I want to take care of you." He laid a gentle hand on her shoulder. "Let me."

A shiver coursed through her, strong enough he felt it. For a moment, her eyes locked with his, letting him experience the moment she accepted not only his offer but something more. "Yes. Please."

Desire slammed into him like a runaway comet. She had given him the gift of trust, a momentary surrender of control. He untangled her hair with care, combing his fingers through her unruly locks a bit at a time. When he was done, he moved on to a scalp massage.

She uttered a low moan of pleasure and sank deeper into the chair as he continued his work. Tariq passed by, moving as quietly as he could on his way to the kitchen. Lunch was the next item on their list.

Jody stirred a few minutes later. "That feels

wonderful. I didn't even realize how stressed I was until you started doing that. You don't have to do it anymore, though. I'm alright now."

"Even if you had nanotech, I wouldn't believe you. You've had a rough morning, and I suspect your mind hasn't finished processing everything. As a healer, my recommendation is to rest and let us take care of you."

She opened her eyes and tipped her head back until she could see him. "I'm a doctor, too. I think I need to get back on my feet and find something useful to do."

Tariq reappeared from the kitchen with a glass of fruit juice in one hand and a glass of water in the other. "Your opinion has been noted and overruled," he said. Once he was close enough, he set both glasses down in front of her. "You need to drink something that isn't full of stimulants."

"Have any of your patients ever mentioned you're a bit bossy?" she asked, selecting the glass of juice.

"Occasionally. Usually they're the stubborn ones who ignore my advice and inevitably wind up needing longer to recover," Tariq said.

"Besides, you already agreed to let us take care of you." Sulat slid his hands down to her shoulders in a slow caress as he lowered his mouth to her ear. "You know what I want to hear."

She shivered, her next breath coming with a soft gasp. "I..."

Tariq dropped to his knees at her feet, his hands resting on her thighs. "Let us do this for you, Jody."

She looked up at him and then down at Tariq, eyes

wide, her entire body trembling now. "If I say yes. What happens?"

"Anything you want," Tariq told her.

"All you have to do is say yes."

Jody closed her eyes and blew out a long, soft breath. "Yes."

"Come with me." Tariq rose to his feet looking like a male reborn. Sulat hadn't seen this side of his *anrik* in far too long. Confident. Eager. Happy. It was good to see him this way.

"Where are we going?" Jody asked, her voice softer than normal.

"To see to your needs," Tariq said and then lifted her high enough he could kiss her, cutting off any more questions.

"Shower or bed?" Tariq sent the question through their link.

"Shower first. Our blossom needs more time to unwind. Can you feel how tense she is?"

"I can. How do humans cope without nanotech to help them manage bio-chemical responses?"

"I suspect they're even more stubborn than you are," Sulat said.

Tariq set Jody down once they reached the main bathing room. Like the rest of the house, it was a large, airy space with a shower large enough to accommodate a full-grown male Vardarian with their wings stretched out or several of them if they kept their wings furled.

Jody took a quick glance around and then looked straight at him. Sulat felt the heat in her gray-eyed gaze flowing over him like molten silver. *Qarf*, she was beautiful.

The tip of her tongue darted out to wet her lower lip, making him think of what it would be like when she had his cock in her mouth and that tongue was stroking his shaft. *Not yet*. They had promises to keep.

They moved toward her at the same time, taking up position on either side.

"Undress him," Sulat instructed as he pointed at Tariq.

Jody looked like she'd been offered a plate full of cookies. "Yes."

Sulat stood and watched as she put her soft hands on his *anrik*, stroking him as she worked out how to unfasten the clasp on his top. Once her hands were busy, he reached in and began undoing the buttons on her shirt. With each glimpse of her bare skin, he moved faster until he finally gave up and tore away the last few fastenings with one tug.

"Hey! I barely have any clothing left as it is," Jody protested.

"We'll buy you new ones... Vardarian outfits designed for easy access." He freed her of the shirt one arm at a time and tossed it aside. "No more buttons."

Her pants were more sensible, held up by a simple knot it took mere seconds to undo. Once they'd slid over her hips, Sulat stood back to enjoy the view.

She was stunning. Her normal attire did nothing to accentuate her natural curves. Without them, she looked even more desirable. Beneath the creamy white silk of her undergarments, he could see the darker skin of her nipples.

He buried his head between her breasts, breathing in the scent of her body as his cock throbbed in time to his heartbeat. All attempts at coordination quickly fell into chaos with both he and Tariq focusing on the nearly naked beauty standing in front of them.

Once they had her stripped bare, Tariq let her finish undressing him before guiding her toward the shower. Sulat stripped off quickly, determined not to be left out.

"Activate shower in the main bathing area. Setting four. Unlimited duration," Tariq issued the command to the house AI. Water immediately fell from the overhead fixture as well as several smaller ones set into the walls.

"I see that being the lead healer has some perks," Jody laughed as she stepped into the center of the jets, a move that shrouded her body in steam.

"And they're all yours, any time you like," Tariq said.

She made a soft, happy sound in the back of her throat. "You make it sound so easy."

"Easy?" Sulat stroked her cheek as she leaned against Tariq. "It won't always be easy. But let's start by showing you how good it can be."

∼

Jody wanted to pinch herself to make sure she wasn't dreaming. So many years of going it alone, of always being the one supporting others without ever really getting that support back. Now Tariq and Sulat were here, offering her something she'd never had before—a chance to be the center of someone's attention. She could be the focus of these two amazing, handsome males who wanted nothing more than to protect and care for her. All she had to do was say yes.

"Yes." She didn't intend to say the word out loud, but some part of her needed to say it again. She didn't know what the future would bring, but right now, all she could feel was the glorious potential that lay ahead of them, and the only answer she could give was *yes*.

She fell into Sulat's arms, kissing him with all the needs of her body and all the hope in her heart. Tariq moved with her, the three of them entwined like some kind of erotic statue in the center of a fountain.

She moved between them, kissing one and then the other. A hand stroked her back, her hips, her breasts, the sensations blurring until she couldn't tell their touches apart. She felt like a goddess, each kiss a promise of devotion, each touch a silent prayer.

Again, her mind whispered a single word that resonated down to her soul. *Yes.*

∼

Every cell in Tariq's body hummed with need. His cock had been hard from the moment he took flight with her in his arms, his mind already full of all the things he wanted to do to her once they were home. He was almost drunk with desire, which was something he'd never expected to feel again. He'd expected at least a few pangs of guilt, but none came. There was only the ache in his balls and a hunger only one thing could sate.

When he couldn't hold back any longer, he drew Jody into his arms, turning her so that she faced him. Water streamed down her face as she looked up at him with a look of trust in her lovely eyes.

"What do you need?" he asked her.

"You. Both of you." She splayed her hands across his chest. "I want to forget about everything else and just be here with you."

Sulat groaned in approval, the big male's eyes closing as he rubbed himself against Jody's back.

"If you get first thrust, I get first taste," Sulat said, never opening his eyes.

"Then you best move your ass. I'm running out of patience."

Sulat laughed and dropped to his knees behind Jody. Tariq knew what came next. Without a word, he reached down and caught one of her legs above the knee, drawing it upward to hold it by his hip.

"What are..." Jody asked but then her lips parted in a sweet moan as Sulat pressed his mouth to her pussy.

"Oh. Oh gods." She gasped and trembled, clinging to Tariq, her eyes closing in pleasure.

He held her steady, enjoying her breathless cries as his partner took her to the heights of pleasure. Every sound buzzed against his tongue as he kissed her. Her nails scored his chest as the pleasure intensified, their kisses growing wilder.

When she came, he captured the sound with his mouth, relishing the way she writhed and quivered against him.

"More?" he asked, ignoring the fact Sulat still had

Chapter 10

two fingers inside her pussy, working her clit and drawing out the last pulses of her orgasm.

"Yes," she whispered against his lips.

Sulat got to his feet, a satisfied smile on his face. "Come here, *zurya*."

Her brow furrowed with confusion, but she obeyed. Normally that was more Sulat's thing, but today that small act of submission made his cock twitch.

Sulat kissed her once, letting the traces of her essence paint her lips before he turned her around to face away from him. "Trust us."

"I do," she said. Then she leaned against him as if she understood what would happen next.

They lifted her into the air, giving her time to wrap her legs around his waist and settle her arms over his shoulders. Once she was comfortable, Tariq let Sulat take her weight as he slid a hand between their bodies to toy with her clit.

She was still sensitive from her first orgasm, so much so it only took a few strokes of his fingers to make her quiver and moan again. "You have no idea how much I like hearing your pleasure. Before we leave this shower, I intend to have you screaming my name."

She bit her lower lip and nodded once before smiling up at him. "Oh, yes, please."

Gently and oh so slowly, he positioned the thick head of his cock against her pussy, rubbing the tip over her clit until she was breathless and squirming between them.

"Now?" Sulat asked.

"Now." The word came out between gritted teeth as he fought to hold back for a few more seconds. Sulat steadied her as she came down around his cock, driving him into the tight heat of her body.

Tariq kept the pads of two fingers over her clit, the pressure eliciting little gasps of pleasure that filled him with delight. He was balls-deep inside her, and she returned the favor by flexing her inner walls around him, pushing his control to the breaking point—and then past it.

He fucked her hard, hands on her hips, rewarding her every moan and whisper with another thrust or stroke of his fingers over her clit. Feet braced, lips locked to hers, he chased her up the peaks of pleasure.

Sulat grunted, his hips rocking as he ground his cock against her backside. It was an intimate dance for three, all of them reaching for release together.

Sulat came first, his primal roar bouncing off the tiled surface of the shower as he emptied himself across Jody's back.

Then it was just the two of them, her mouth on his, her legs gripping his hips as she rode his cock hard. He felt her orgasm build, each thrust pushing her closer, her cries getting louder, until she threw her head back and called his name as her body pulsed and fluttered around his cock.

His orgasm tore through him with the force of an explosion, driving the air from his lungs as he groaned and shuddered again and again, his swollen cock jerking in time with his hips.

They stood together for a few more seconds, everyone too breathless to speak. Then Jody giggled and turned so she could look at them both at once. "I really could get used to this."

Sulat reached up to sweep her hair back from her face as Tariq held her close. "All you have to do is ask."

He leaned in to nuzzle her cheek. "Or you can just say yes. I'm growing quite fond of that word."

11

Jody wasn't used to sitting around with nothing to do. Her standard approach to any crisis was usually to jump in with both feet and figure things out she went. This time, things were different. Staying out of sight was the best thing she could do, not only for her own safety, but to give Yardan and his people time to do their work without disruption. Knowing that made it easier to stay away, but she still didn't like it.

Sulat and Tariq did all they could to help her deal with the situation. They were kind, patient, and attentive in ways she'd never expected or experienced before. It was a relief to walk out from under the day-to-day burdens of responsibility she'd carried for so long. Of course, she still had plenty of things to worry about. She'd lost her home and most of her possessions while a group of hate-fueled assholes were doing their best to run her out of the colony.

The first day had passed with almost no news. She'd

kept in contact with Lores while her lovers exchanged updates with their daughter and the other healers.

The two males organized a delivery of basic personal items to be sent over and left with the guards outside. Vixi and the other women in the camp went through their closets to assemble several outfits for Jody to wear until she could buy her own.

A cyborg named Shadow volunteered to bring it over, and the arrival of the former assassin proved to be a pleasant but brief distraction. It also reminded Jody that her friends were more than capable of taking care of themselves and each other.

As the hours passed, word of the incidents spread. Messages of support were posted along with offers of assistance from businesses around the colony. The generosity and kindness were balms to her soul.

She'd come here unsure of what she wanted her future to look like. Now she understood what she'd been looking for. *This*. Not just Sulat and Tariq and her hopes that they had a real chance at a future together. She wanted a sense of belonging, of community. She wanted a *home*, and Haven was it.

At her request, the evening meal was a joint effort. Cooking together proved to be a fun, relaxing way to pass the time. She and Sulat each cooked one of their favorite comfort foods while Tariq put together a dessert that featured dozens of thin wafer cookies layered with a creamy, whipped concoction she sampled every time his back was turned. They laughed and got in each other's way, creating a small circle of light and joy that kept the darkness at bay.

Like everything else in her life, she didn't know if it would last, but she intended to hold on to it as long as she could.

By the next morning, the lack of information had them all uneasy again. Jody had hoped this would all be resolved quickly. The only word they had from Yardan was to stay put, be patient, and ignore anything that didn't come directly from him or Skye.

"This waiting around is making me crazy," she announced after taking yet another aimless walk around her temporary home.

"What would help?" Tariq asked. The two males were seated in the living room, both reading on their data tablets.

Sulat glanced up from his tablet with gleaming eyes and a wicked smile. She recognized the look and knew exactly what the randy male would suggest as a distraction. "No, Sulat, that wasn't a request to go back to bed. Or the shower. Or the couch."

Tariq chuckled. "What about the kitchen table? We've only abused that piece of furniture once."

Tariq's dessert had been a key element in that bout of love-making, and she blushed at the recollection. "Maybe later."

Sulat got to his feet. "I've got an idea. Be right back."

She watched him take to the air and fly up to the second floor instead of using the stairs. *That* would take some getting used to.

"Any idea what he's up to?" she asked Tariq.

"Yes."

"Care to elaborate?"

Tariq smiled, his green eyes dancing with mirth. "No. But I'd suggest you stay on your feet while you wait to find out."

"Does this involve nudity, cookies, or both?" she asked.

"Neither. Unless he's deviating from the plan."

That got her attention. "There's a plan?"

"Mhmm." Tariq rose, stretched, and sauntered over to where she stood. "We've talked a great deal in the last week. About the past, where we are now..." He brushed a kiss to the crown of her head. "And what our future might hold. We talked again last night after you were asleep."

A buzz of anticipation filled her mind along with a dozen or so questions. Before she had time to ask any of them, Sulat reappeared. He hopped the railing, wings unfurled to slow his fall. The floor shook with the impact of his landing.

"Was that necessary?" Tariq asked.

"No, but it was fun," Sulat said. He walked into the living area and then dropped to his knees at her feet.

Tariq joined him, leaving her standing in front of two bare-chested males with upturned faces and hopeful smiles.

Uncertain what to do, Jody let the moment play out. After a short pause, Sulat reached down to pull a dagger from his belt. It was smaller than the one she'd seen him with yesterday, and the blade appeared to be inlaid with gold letters she couldn't read.

Without a word, he held the dagger out hilt first. Tariq set his hand over Sulat's, making it an offering from them both. It only took a second for her to recognize the gesture and what it meant.

This was a mating ritual. The blade represented a declaration of intent and a promise of their protection.

She reached out and then froze, her hand still outstretched. "I don't understand. I'm not your *mahaya*."

"No, you're not," Tariq said, his voice solemn. "You are something else. An unexpected gift." His eyes met hers. "But I'd be ten kinds of a fool to let you go."

"Instead of the five or six kinds of fool he was to resist the inevitable as long as he did," Sulat said. The comment earned him a wing bash from his *anrik*.

"But this..." she touched the bare blade with care. "I know what it means. Are you sure you want to make that kind of promise?"

Sulat huffed a laugh. "Would we be on our knees if we weren't certain?"

"I suppose not. But this is all happening rather quickly. Isn't it?"

"Not for us. I don't know what this is or how it happened, but what we have between us is... More..." Sulat waved a hand in the air in front of him. "I'm trying to find words the translator will understand. You are a fire in my blood. It's been that way since our first kiss. I cannot get you out of my mind, Jody. This feels different. Stronger."

"We're meant to be together. I feel it in here." Tariq tapped his chest with his free hand.

So she wasn't the only one who felt it. The more time she spent with them, the more complete she felt—not only the physical pleasure but a soul-deep connection.

She'd thought it was wishful thinking on her part, but it wasn't.

"I feel that, too," she admitted. Then she asked, "So, now what?"

"Now is the time to say my favorite word," Tariq coaxed.

"And accept our gift," Sulat added.

She took the dagger, smiled, and uttered the word that brought her so much happiness. "Yes."

～

Tariq's happiness was a tangible thing, lightening his steps as well as his spirit. Despite the challenges of the last few days and the many that still lay ahead of them, he couldn't stop smiling. He even looked forward to telling Vixi that she'd been right about Jody, despite the gloating their little whirlwind would do once she heard.

He and Sulat had talked for hours last night as Jody slept between them, too exhausted for their quiet conversation to disturb her rest.

Both of them were experiencing the same thing—a visceral, undeniable attraction that strengthened by the hour. It wasn't the *sharhal*, the mating fever that only came once in a lifetime, but it was something close to it.

Looking back, he could see his interest had grown despite his anger and guilt, but those feelings couldn't compare to what he felt once they'd kissed.

Those feelings couldn't be ignored. Not that either of them wanted to. Neither of them understood how this could be happening, but understanding would have to wait. For now, they needed to focus on keeping her safe while making her understand that she was a part of their lives now and forever more.

The blade they gave her was one of his, an heirloom handed down to him by his father, and it looked good in Jody's hand. Not that she'd ever need to use it. It was a symbolic gift but an important one.

The next step would take more time and require an important conversation. Claiming Jody involved mating marks and an exchange of nanotech. Once bitten, she'd carry that tech for the rest of what should be a very long life, longer than that of her son and any normal humans she knew. For now, it was enough that she had accepted their blade and the promises that went with it.

His good mood lasted until late afternoon. Local forecasts predicted a storm was headed this way, the first in a series that might last the better part of a day.

He hated storms now. Every gust of wind and boom of thunder brought back dark memories. Even now, with hope in his heart and Jody by his side, he knew the next few hours wouldn't be easy.

Normally he'd retreat to his reading nook, opaque the window to blot out the view, and try to drown out the thunder and wind with music. It never worked and left him feeling even more isolated, so today he joined Jody on the couch.

"Did you hear from Vixi? Is something wrong?" she asked the moment she looked up from the tablet she'd been reading.

"There's nothing new to report. I wish I had good news to share, but at least there's no bad news either."

She frowned and laid a hand on his arm. "Then what's wrong?"

Talking about it was the last thing he wanted to do, but she needed to know. "Bad memories," he told her. "Raenia died when we were caught in a storm. Days like this take me back to the moment it happened."

She took his hand and squeezed it hard. "I hate storms, too. Always have. It's all too loud and violent for me. I swear a storm sent me into premature labor with Jacob. I was home alone, trying not to think about the chaos outside, when lightning struck the building. The power went out, the whole building shook, and I was so scared..." She snuggled in beside him. "By the time the skies cleared, Jacob was on his way into this world."

"Where was your mate?" he asked.

"Gone. Kyle volunteered for mission of some kind, a plum assignment, he called it. An opportunity he couldn't pass up. He went even though it meant leaving me alone a month before our baby was due. He promised he'd be back before the big day, but of course he wasn't. Jacob was ten weeks old when he came home, and by the time he could crawl, Kyle was gone again."

"He didn't deserve you," Tariq muttered.

"He didn't love me," she corrected him. "Oh, he thought he did, but he only loved the idea of a wife. His one true love was, and still is, the military. He's not a bad man. Just a bad husband." She sighed. "And lousy father, which is why it annoys me that Jacob joined the military. I know it's his way of trying to get Kyle's approval."

Tariq thought about Vixi and how often he wished

she'd chosen a safer path for herself. "As much as we hate it, we have to let them make their own decisions."

She laughed. "I won't tell Vixi you said that."

"Please don't. I'd never hear the end of it."

Their conversation helped, and when the first clap of thunder boomed overhead, it didn't make him jump the way it used to. Given time, he'd get over this too. So long as he never had to fly into a storm again.

He scoffed at the thought. Nothing on the planet could get him outside on a day like this.

12

"Now? Okay. How is she doing? How far apart are the contractions?" Jody's question roused Tariq from sleep. He blinked, stretched, and was about to ask what was going on when Jody's question finally sank into his sleep-fuddled brain. Contractions.

He scrambled to his feet as the adrenaline kicked in. They only had one pregnant patient at the moment. Phaedra.

"Okay. That's good. We still have plenty of time. We'll take a transport to the palace right away. The rangers standing guard outside can come with us."

Jody stood near the foot of his bed, her naked body briefly outlined by a bolt of lightning visible through the window.

Sulat was beside her, both of them looking at the vidscreen of her comm device. A male voice came out of the speaker, but the words were impossible to make out at this distance.

"What do you mean she's not there?" Jody scowled at the screen.

The same someone replied, and this time he heard enough to recognize the speaker: Prince Tyran.

"Need to know? We're her medical team. Of course we should have been told! If anyone had bothered to ask, I'd have informed them that moving Phaedra this close to her due date was a bad idea."

More information from Tyran, who sounded even more worried than he had the other night.

"Well, it's too late now." Jody pinched the bridge of her nose as if staving off a headache. "We'll have to come to you."

By this time, Tariq had moved close enough to hear both sides of the conversation.

"The storm's expected to intensify. The entire fleet is grounded for the time being." Tyran stared up at Jody with a look of utter frustration. "There was an attack inside the palace walls. Someone on the inside is working with the *Liq'za*. Most of the palace staff are currently being interviewed, and I suspect that's too gentle a word for what Yardan is putting them through."

Jody blew out a long breath. "Alright. I see why you moved her. I'm not happy about it, but that's a conversation for another time. For now, I need you to tell me one thing, and I don't care that this is a potentially insecure connection."

Tyran nodded. "Whatever you need."

"Tell me where the *fraxx* you took my patient!"

"I can't do that," Tyran said.

Sulat took the comm device from Jody, who seemed

to have lost the ability to speak. "Why not?" he demanded.

"I don't actually know. We were forced to land before the storm tore our shuttle apart. Braxon is piloting and knows where we are. I'll get him to forward the coordinates to you."

"Thank you. Before you do that, I need to know what medical equipment you have on board and who else is with you."

"Several of my personal guards are here, and I know none of them are with the *Liq'za*. Other than that, it's just the three of us." Tyran paled slightly as Phaedra cried out in pain. "Soon to be four of us."

The call ended, leaving the three of them staring at each other.

"Any thoughts on how we're going to reach them in time?" Jody asked.

"We could drive," Tariq said.

The screen flashed again, this time with a text message. Sulat read it and cursed. "No, we can't. They must have been headed over the mountains to Raze's place, but they couldn't get there." He pointed to the screen. "They're in the foothills, here. We'd never get to them in time. No roads that far out, and the woods are too thick to drive through."

"Air bikes?" Tariq suggested and then shook his head. "Forget that idea. Those things aren't stable enough to fly in this weather."

Sulat looked at him in horror. "I can't believe you even suggested it."

"I said forget it." They were bantering now because

both of them knew what had to happen, and neither wanted to be the first to say it.

"There's only one way. Isn't there?" Jody asked, her voice low but determined.

"There is." Sulat agreed. "But not all of us need to take the risk. I can go. You stay here with Tariq. I'll contact you when I reach them, and you can walk me through whatever needs to be done."

"I'll go. You're a good healer, but your specialty has always been research. Besides," Tariq tried to sound cocky, "the princess likes me better than you."

Jody stepped between them. "No. I need to be there in person. Phaedra's vitals are still in the normal range, but my gut tells me something's wrong."

Both men opened their mouths but then closed them at the same time. Jody was right, which meant there was no point in wasting time with an argument they already knew they'd lose.

"You will fly with Sulat," Tariq told her. "I will carry the equipment."

He moved close enough to his anrik to clasp his shoulder. "Take care of her. I will do my best to keep up."

"You *will* keep up. If we're doing this, we do it together." She caught both their hands and drew them in close. "It's too soon for this conversation, but since we're about to do something completely inadvisable, I'm going to say it anyway. I don't love you yet, but it's inevitable. So, let's get this over with and go back to living a nice, safe life together."

Tariq pretended not to notice the way Jody's hand

shook or the slight tremor in her voice as she spoke. "Together," he repeated, making the word into a vow.

"Together. Always," Sulat said.

Five minutes later, the three of them headed out into the storm.

∼

This flight was nothing like the last time she'd flown with Sulat. There was no warm summer breeze, no stars overhead, and no pretty lights twinkling below.

The wind shrieked around them like a living thing, battering them with gusts that tore at her clothes and skin and pummeled her with rain. The straps that linked her harness to his were so slick she couldn't keep hold of them. Though maybe that was because her fingers were so cold she couldn't feel them anymore.

Lightning raced across the sky like streaks of white fire, leaping between the clouds. The brilliant light blinded her, and the rain made it difficult to see anything in the all-consuming darkness. But she kept her eyes open anyway. Tariq was somewhere out there, though she never saw him for more than a second at a time. Sometimes he was above them, only to appear below the next time she caught a glimpse of him.

Peals of thunder boomed and cracked so loudly they shook them both.

Speaking was impossible, but Sulat would touch her face from time to time, the only comfort he could offer while he struggled to navigate the maelstrom.

The rain lightened after what felt like an eternity,

allowing her to see a little better. A distant flash of lightning danced on the horizon, providing enough light for her to see Tariq. He flew to their right, his head bowed against the wind.

When he dropped into a sudden dive, she cried out in fear, reaching out as if she could somehow stop him from falling. She cried out again when Sulat followed him, rushing toward the ground and a tiny cluster of lights.

Lights! Was that the shuttle? *Please be the shuttle. Please, please, please.*

They landed in the same clearing as the shuttle, both males stumbling as they impacted the muddy terrain.

Jody tried to unfasten the harness straps, but her hands were like ice blocks, and she couldn't stop her teeth from chattering. They'd outfitted her as best they could for the weather, but their boots and gloves were too big and would have been more hinderance than help.

"You holding up?" Sulat asked as he pulled off his gloves to get to the straps.

She ignored his attempts to free her and pulled herself up to kiss him.

"Cold. Wet. Thankful to be back on th-the ground."

He kissed her back, his lips as cold as hers, though the touch of his mouth helped to warm her in ways that had nothing to do with skin temperature.

"And to think I used to storm-dive for fun. My younger self was an idiot," he said.

"For fun?" she asked. "What about that ordeal was supposed to be the fun part?"

"I can't remember," Sulat admitted.

Tariq appeared, lugging the gear he'd carried. "Me either. Let's get inside and out of this *fraxxing* awful storm."

The moment she was free of the harness, she ran to Tariq and threw her arms around him. "You're okay?" she asked.

"I'm fine, *zurya*." He leaned down to kiss her, one hand sweeping the sodden mess of her hair out of her eyes.

"We did it. And I never want to do that again."

"Agreed."

A shaft of warm, welcoming light streamed out of the darkness, and Tyran's voice called over the noise of the storm. "You're all insane, and I'm grateful. Now, please hurry."

"Royal gratitude sounds good," Sulat muttered as they stumbled toward the shuttle. "Do you think it comes with better pay?"

"And cookies," Jody said. "A lifetime supply."

13

It turned out that delivering a breech baby was easier than flying through a thunderstorm, though Tariq doubted Phaedra felt the same way.

A combination of issues complicated the delivery, but they had prepared for most of them. The greatest challenge had been to keep the fathers calm and focused on Phaedra while the three healers worked in the cramped cabin of the shuttle.

By the time the child was born, the storm was over and the first rays of dawn reached up into a clear blue sky. Once mother and daughter were examined and declared healthy, the three of them had gone outside. The new family needed some time alone, so they and the guards had stepped out to watch the sunrise and wait for their ride to arrive.

Yardan himself piloted the ship that brought them back to Haven, and he had news to share.

"We haven't got them all yet, but once one broke

down and gave us a name, it didn't take long to gather up most of them."

"How can you know you have most of them when we don't know how many there are?" Jody asked, her voice thick with exhaustion.

"We can't," Yardan admitted. "But Haven's not a big colony, and I cannot imagine too many of them are *Liq'za*. A few of them aren't even citizens. They came in on a Vardarian cargo ship a week ago. The ship is undergoing a refit, and these *bakaffa* were here to relax for a few weeks before heading out again. They were hired help with no idea what they'd signed up for."

"So it's safe for everyone to return home now?" Jody asked.

"In a day or so. I want to be sure. The palace staff have all been cleared, though I have some concerns about a few. They're all being transferred to other assignments for now. Nothing near the palace."

"You think one of them let the *Liq'za* in?" Tariq asked.

"I think at least one of them is part of the group." Yardan scrubbed a hand over his beard. "This is a *fraxxing* mess, and cleaning it up will take time."

"But for now, we're safe." Jody nestled a little deeper into her chair, her eyes already closing as the events of the night caught up to her.

"You're safe, Jody. We'll make sure of it," Tariq promised her.

Sulat smiled and placed his hand on Tariq's shoulder. "Yes, we will."

Once home, they all went straight to bed. Even with

Chapter 13

nanotech enhancements, he and Sulat needed sleep, though not nearly as much as Jody did.

Hours later he sat in the kitchen with his *anrik* drinking freshly brewed *kabari*.

"Do you think she'll sleep all night?" Sulat asked.

"I doubt it. I assume she'll wake up soon, even if it's just to eat and hydrate."

"I hate knowing she's so vulnerable," Sulat blurted out a moment later.

"I know." It worried him, too. Accelerated healing was something most Vardarians took for granted along with improved strength and endurance.

The solution was obvious, but it had to be her decision.

"We talked about this already and both agreed we shouldn't rush her decision." Sulat sighed and rubbed the back of his neck. "But..."

"But she'd be safer if she had the tech," Tariq finished the thought. "It's more than that, though. I need to protect her every way I can. I need her in every way possible."

He hadn't put his feelings into words until now, but hearing them aloud made it so obvious. "I want to claim her, Sulat. That shouldn't be possible."

Sulat grunted. "I know. I feel it too, and it's getting stronger."

"It is. But it's all in our heads. It has to be."

"I'm not sure about that. I have a theory." Sulat set down his mug. "I'll need a blood sample, though."

"A blood sample. Why?"

"Because if I'm right, I get to write a medical paper

that will earn me accolades across the empire." Sulat grinned. "Did any of your mentors ever mention the *sharhal-li?*"

"The echo of mating fever? That's just a legend. There's no scientific proof it has ever happened or could happen. The *sharhal* only happens once in a lifetime."

"That's why I want blood samples. If you and I both have the markers of the *sharhal*, even in trace amounts, it means there's something to the stories."

"That is an interesting theory. Please tell me you have what you need to run the tests here because there's no way we're waking Jody up unless we're certain."

Sulat grinned so widely his fangs showed. "Of course I do."

"Then let's find out." No matter what the tests showed, his feelings for Jody wouldn't change. But if he and Sulat were experiencing the *sharhal-li*, it was a blessing from their ancestors and, perhaps, a message from Raenia. It was time for them to move on.

∼

Jody finished her meal and pushed back her plate with a dramatic flourish. "There. I've eaten. I took the supplements, and I finished my glass of water. Now will you please tell me what the *fraxx* is going on?"

As amusing as it was to watch the two of them try and pretend to be calm, she wanted to know what had happened.

"What makes you think that?" Sulat asked.

"Well, for starters, you keep flicking your wings, and

Chapter 13

Tariq hasn't stopped prowling around the room since I sat down. I trust you would have told me if there was bad news, so this must be something else."

"You belong with us," Sulat said, his voice low and possessive.

"In our home. In our lives. In our bed," Tariq continued.

She wanted to say yes and skip straight to whatever came next, but she couldn't. "Are you sure? I mean, I know what I want, but it's still early in our relationship. There's no reason to rush things."

She hated herself for saying it. She *wanted* to rush headlong into this adventure.

"We're sure," Tariq said, his eyes gleaming with desire.

"Very," Sulat said. "You are our female, and so much more. There's no word for what you are because there's never been proof this kind of thing was possible. But it is. And you are."

Jody couldn't work out what they were talking about. "I think I'm missing something here, and I get the feeling it's important. What are you saying?"

"We are both experiencing the *sharhal-li*. Think of it as an echo of the full mating fever."

They both moved to stand on either side of her, their hands on her shoulders. "You're ours, Jody. And we are yours."

"I didn't know that was possible." She dredged the words out of the tangled wreckage of her thoughts. Joy and wonder filled her along with a dozen questions she'd save for another time.

"It's rare. So rare there's never been a certified case. But there are stories, and now we know they are true," Tariq said.

"Blood tested and verified," Sulat confirmed.

"Wow." She reached up to clutch their hands as the news sank in. "So, we're mated?"

"Not yet." Tariq brushed her hair back from her shoulder, his fingers stroking the side of her throat. "That normally involves an exchange of mating marks."

She understood immediately. "And that means I'd carry your nanotech. I'd be like you."

"It's your decision, *zurya*. We want you as our mate in every way, but it's not up to us. If you wish to wait, we understand," Sulat said.

"My choice." She took a breath and broke into joyous laughter as she gave them her answer. "Yes."

Euphoric chaos erupted after that. She was out of her seat in seconds, only to be lifted into the air and spun around. Laughter filled her ears and happiness swelled in her chest.

The next thing she knew, Tariq had her pinned against a wall, his mouth on hers. His hands deftly released the fastenings on the Vardarian dress she'd opted to wear.

"I'm starting to see the appeal of these outfits," she whispered between kisses.

Tariq's only reply was a low groan of raw need. His hard body pressed tightly against hers as he ground the hard bar of his cock into her stomach.

"You could make it easier still by staying naked whenever we're alone," Sulat suggested. He stood close enough to touch. Somehow he'd managed to undress already, his scales gleaming bright with desire.

As tempting as the idea was, she saw a major flaw with it. "If I did that, we'd never accomplish anything."

"I can think of a few things we'd do quite a bit of," Sulat argued.

Tariq raised his head and turned to flash his fangs at his *anrik*. "Less talking, more doing."

"And I thought Sulat was the one who liked to be in control," she sassed.

"He's no more in control right now than I am." Tariq caught her hand and dragged it down to his cock. "I want you. He wants you. We are going to take you, claim you, and mark you as ours forever."

His words came out as a growl that soaked her pussy and made her pulse race with desire. "Yes. Oh *fraxx*, yes." She recalled the conversation with the new arrivals not very long ago and chuckled. "I hope you have *uli* oil in the house."

In response, Tariq's cock twitched and Sulat's voice dropped to a low rumble. "Together?" he asked.

"Yes," she said. *Veth*. She really liked that word. It had led her to this impossibly improbable place where her dreams—and several wicked fantasies—would all come true.

Hard, heated skin moved beneath her hands as Tariq lifted her into the air. "Hold on, *zurya*. We're moving to somewhere more comfortable."

She expected him to carry her upstairs, but they didn't make it that far. Instead, he stopped at the first couch he came to and fell backward onto it, taking her with her.

She landed on top of him, laughing and breathless, his cock trapped beneath her as she deliberately wriggled and pretended to try and get up.

He caught her easily, pulling her down for a long, deep kiss. His mouth savaged hers, his fangs grazing her lips and the tips sharp enough to draw blood. She didn't care. Instead, she nipped his lower lip, her fingers raking through his hair.

She rubbed her pussy over his hard shaft, needing something to take the edge off her throbbing clit. Knowing this was some variation of the mating fever was freeing. It meant she could indulge herself in every way she'd ever wanted.

Tariq's kisses grew harder, his tongue plunging into her mouth as he fisted one hand in her hair.

A whoosh of air alerted her to Sulat's return.

"Where?" she asked, the single word all her brain could manage.

"Uli oil, as requested," he said and settled in behind her. His weight made the cushions dip.

"Who told you about that?" Tariq asked, his voice a whisper against her lips.

Jody lifted her head just enough to look at him properly and saw a flash of jealousy in his gorgeous green eyes.

"I read about it while learning what I could about Vardarian mating rituals. It came up in a session I taught last week. The women were very interested in how this might work."

Chapter 13

Sulat's fingers traced a pattern across the small of her back. "That's a good answer. It means you've never experienced it for yourself." His hand slipped lower, along the seam of her ass and down to her pussy.

The skin he touched tingled, the sensation increasing the longer the oil lingered on her skin. She moaned as the feeling intensified, muffling the sound against Tariq's mouth.

An oil-slick hand slipped between her body and Tariq's, seeking out her nipples one at a time. Every tweak and touch added to her arousal. In a matter of seconds, she was writhing between them as they caressed her with hard, urgent hands.

Sulat coaxed her onto her hands and knees and away from the throbbing length of Tariq's cock. Once she was clear, he used his fingers to coat her pussy with the oil, making sure to make several tight circles around her clit.

Tariq uttered a groan as some of the oil dripped off Sulat's hand and onto his cock. His next breath hissed across his teeth, and he raised his hips to grind against both her cunt and Sulat's fingers.

"Nope. First she comes, then we do. You can wait, Riq." Sulat's comment made her giggle. Breaking her kiss, she turned to look over her shoulder at Sulat as he knelt behind her. He winked at her as if he knew exactly what she was thinking as he strummed her clit with his fingers.

She shivered and bucked against Sulat's touch. She ached with need, not for one cock but for two. She wanted them both inside her. Now.

Sulat worked her clit hard for several strokes,

bringing her to the brink of orgasm before pulling his hand away.

She lowered herself onto Tariq's cock a second later, earning herself a grin from the male lying beneath her.

"I don't think she wants to wait, and I know I don't." Tariq arched himself beneath her, letting his cock slide between her folds, the oil making everything more intense.

"Do you want my cock, *zurya*?" he asked in a voice gone rough with need.

"You know the answer to that will always be yes."

"I do. But I like hearing you say it." He released her breast and reached between them, seating the thick head of his cock at her opening.

She didn't wait for him to move his hand but drove herself down on his cock, taking him balls deep inside her.

"Qarf!" Tariq's hips snapped up, the sound of tearing fabric filling the air as he ripped the couch cushion with his fingers.

Jody's mind and body were bombarded with sensations so intense they threatened to overwhelm her. Her skin burned as her pussy throbbed and pulsed around Tariq's cock.

Behind her, Sulat worked his fingers into the cleft of her ass, more oil coating his fingers as he slowly worked his way deeper.

When he penetrated her from behind, she stiffened, not with pain but a new, darker kind of pleasure. He worked her slowly open, each press of his fingers driving her down onto Tariq's cock.

Chapter 13

The tempo slowed as the intensity increased, riding wave after wave of pleasure.

When Sulat pulled his hand away this time, she knew what would happen next. Despite herself, she tensed and uttered a low, needy moan.

Tariq touched her cheek, drawing her attention back to him. "Trust comes before submission," he whispered. Sulat had said the same words to her the night of their first kiss.

"You have my trust and my heart. Both of you." Then she allowed herself to relax and trust her lovers to take care of her.

Sulat pressed himself against her back opening, easing himself slowly into the tight ring of her ass. After a bite of pain that faded into pleasure, she was truly caught between them.

She could do nothing but let them love her, each of them moving in turn and taking her to the peaks of ecstasy. One would enter as one retreated.

"So beautiful," Sulat murmured, his hands on her hips as he fucked her.

"Yes, she is," Tariq agreed. "Our *zurya*."

On the last word, he raised his head to kiss the side of her throat. Only it was more than a kiss. As his fangs broke the skin, Sulat leaned over her, claiming the other side of her neck.

Jody's world exploded into crystalline bliss. Her senses shattered as an orgasm stronger than she'd ever experienced tore through her. She lost herself in a sea of pleasure, her body clamping down on both males as they came along with her.

She collapsed onto Tariq with a deep, contented sigh, her body still rocked by aftershocks and her heart overflowing with love.

"Mine," she murmured dazedly, barely aware of the words coming out of her mouth.

"I think that's our line." Sulat chuckled, his breath tickling the back of her neck. "But feel free to keep using it."

"Oh, I plan on it." She let herself linger in post-coital bliss for as long as she could and then sighed as a thought occurred to her.

"You know, the second Yardan gives us the all-clear signal. We're going to have to go back to work."

"Do you think he can be bribed to prolong it a day or two?" Tariq asked. "Because the moment it's safe, Vixi will be over here to check on us."

"What's wrong with that?" Jody asked.

"She's going to be unbelievably smug when she learns we claimed you."

"Your smug daughter I can deal with. Telling Jake I've taken up with two males will be... interesting."

Her mates just laughed. "If he has any concerns, he's welcome to visit us. After all, he's part of the family now."

Family. Yes. She liked the way that sounded. The danger wasn't over, and her new life was just beginning, but Jody had no regrets. She was where she was supposed to be with the males she was destined to love.

∼

Thank You for Reading Her Alien Healers

Chapter 13

I hope you enjoyed Jody, Tariq, and Sulat's story. Would you like to read a special bonus epilogue to this story? Sign up for my newsletter here: subscribepage.io/Bonuscontent

If you're looking for more stories like this one, I invite you to explore the other books in the Drift universe, which now Include Haven Colony, Nova Force and the original Drift series.

ABOUT THE AUTHOR

Susan lives out on the Canadian west coast surrounded by open water, dear family, and good friends. She's jumped out of perfectly good airplanes on purpose and accidentally swum with sharks on the Great Barrier Reef.

If the world ends, she plans to survive as the spunky, comedic sidekick to the heroes of the new world, because she's too damned short and out of shape to make it on her own for long.

You can find out more about Susan and her books at:
www.susanhayes.ca

Printed in Great Britain
by Amazon